BELLA'S HOLIDAY

LEGACY SERIES
BOOK 8

PAULA KAY

DEDICATION

To Gwendolyn.
So happy that our lives have crossed paths.
Your talent has given me more smiles than I can
count as I've listened to my characters come to life.

CONTENTS

ONE

Lia looked across the table at her granddaughter. She couldn't really put her finger on it, but Isabella seemed different somehow. She was smiling and chatting away, but Lia could tell that something wasn't quite right. She reached across the table to place her hand on Isabella's arm.

"Honey, is everything okay?"

Isabella looked confused. "Yeah. Everything's great, why?"

"Oh, I just sense that there's something bothering you. Bella, you know you can talk to me, right?"

Isabella smiled. "Of course. Yes, I do know that and yes, everything is just fine. You have no idea how wonderful it is to be here—sitting in Thyme with you. The restaurant looks great and the food is perfect as usual." Isabella scooped up a forkful of pasta, as if she needed to prove her point.

"Alright then. If you say so. I don't want to nag at all. And you have no idea how wonderful it's going to be to have a house full of people this year for Christmas."

"The villa looks so festive with all the Christmas decorations. Antonio told me how hard you've been working at it all, and I really hope you're not overextending yourself. I mean, I'm sure the restaurant must have you pretty busy this time of year. And now Jemma and I are here to help." Isabella grinned.

"Oh, honestly, I pop in the restaurant whenever I get the urge—"

"—which I'm sure is often." Isabella laughed.

"Well, true." Lia laughed too. "But, Sofia handles everything. Between her and the assistant manager, I could leave Italy for months and no one would ever even know I was gone."

"I'm sure that's not quite true, but I'll keep that in mind. Maybe a trip together in our near future?" Isabella winked.

Something inside of Lia stirred at the mention of a trip with her granddaughter. She had so many beautiful memories of traveling with Isabella's mother, Arianna, before she died. The idea of being able to recreate some of those memories with Isabella was surreal to think about.

"Bella, you have no idea how wonderful that sounds. We just might have to consider that. Oh, and speaking about the decorating, I've left one thing that I thought we could all do together—with the kids."

Isabella grinned. "Does this have to do with the huge tree I saw by the fireplace?"

Lia laughed. "Yes. I sent Antonio out with orders to get the tallest, fullest tree he could find."

"And he delivered." Isabella laughed.

"That he did."

"You and Antonio seem to be doing really well, and I love the additions you've made to the property."

"Yes, that was all Antonio's doing. He said—and I agreed—that he wanted a place where we could have all our friends and family at the villa at the same time. And of course that needs to account for expanded family down the road—all our future grandchildren one day." Lia winked.

Isabella laughed, but Lia thought she noticed a flash of something cross her face.

"One day in the far-off future, I'd say."

"Well, you're young yet, Bella. But one day..."

"Sure. One day. But enough about my future children. When is everyone else arriving?"

"Well, you know your parents arrive tomorrow and Blu and her family the day after. Douglas and—" Lia stopped herself, unsure how much of a secret Douglas's guest was supposed to be.

"Douglas and?" Isabella said.

"Douglas arrives on the weekend—Saturday."

"I'm sure Gigi is missing him terribly." Isabella laughed.

Gigi had arrived the week before and been a big help to Lia with all the decorating and preparations. The two had grown very close over the years and Lia always loved having her at the villa.

"Oh, you know those two—they're still like newlyweds."

Isabella laughed. "You should talk. I've seen the way Antonio looks at you."

Lia felt her face turn warm. "Your grandfather is the best thing that ever happened to me—how I ever got so lucky to get a second chance with him, I'll never understand."

"Well, Antonio says that he's the lucky one."

"Well, we're both lucky, I'd say—and mostly to have a talented beautiful granddaughter such as yourself." Lia smiled at Isabella, willing her to know just how deeply she loved her. "Now, enough talk about us. Bella, tell me about Lucas—and your sister. Oh, the pictures you sent of Thanksgiving were so sweet."

Lia listened to Isabella talk about the meeting with her birth father and family in San Francisco. She loved the way the young girl's face lit up as she talked about her little sister Annie and the time they'd had together. And Isabella shared with Lia how much she'd enjoyed San Francisco—sight-seeing and Christmas shopping with her best friend, Thomas.

Lia had heard a lot about Thomas from the first time Isabella had come to visit them in Tuscany. She knew the young man was one of the most important people in her granddaughter's life, and it was obvious to see that he'd been a huge source of support for Isabella.

"And you said that Thomas won't be able to make it for Christmas after all?"

There was the look. Lia didn't have to wonder as she saw the quick expression cross Isabella's face. Something had happened between her granddaughter and this friend of hers, Thomas.

"No. No, thanks for inviting him, but he's going to stay in London for the holidays." Isabella glanced up at her. "He's got a girlfriend there. But maybe another time you'll be able to meet him."

"I'd like that. Well, he's always welcome—as are any of your friends."

"Thank you."

"Speaking of..."

Isabella looked over at Lia with a question on her face. "Yes?"

"Antonio and I were talking about your father—sorry, about Lucas."

4

Isabella smiled. "I know. It's kinda weird. But right now, he's Lucas. I mean, I have a father and mother. And thank God, they've been so supportive with everything. Or else—well, who knows. Maybe it would have been way harder for me to come and meet you all, had they not accepted everything so well. Not to say I wouldn't have, but you know—it's so much better having everyone's support. And also they love you all as much as I do."

Lia smiled. "We feel the same. Of course. They've done a great job raising our Isabella."

Isabella laughed. "I guess. So, you were saying? About Lucas?"

"Yes, so Antonio and I wanted you to know that you should invite him—and the whole family, of course—for Christmas. If you wanted to, that is."

Isabella's face seemed to light up. "Really? Hm. How would that work? There's not much time, but it would be incredible to have them here."

"Well, logistically, I know Douglas could make it happen—get them on a good flight and everything. It's really up to you—how you feel about it. And I'm guessing that might have to do with your parents."

"Yeah, that's what I was thinking. I'm not quite sure if they're ready for that meeting, but they sure have surprised me these past months."

Lia knew exactly what Isabella meant. Emily and Richard had been fully onboard once their daughter had explained to them why she'd wanted to put Harvard on hold. Receiving Arianna's inheritance had had a big impact on Isabella's life, creating new opportunities for her—just as Lia's own inheritance had done for her so many years earlier. And Emily and

Richard had been very supportive of the decisions their daughter had been making along the way.

"Well, you decide, honey—and just let us know. They are more than welcome, and we've got more than enough room for everyone. I know that Gabriela and Kylie would love having another playmate, and any excuse for me to add place settings to our ever-expanding dining table makes me that much happier."

"Thank you very much. I appreciate the offer. I'm going to think about it and not decide one way or another until my parents arrive. If it feels right, I'll have a conversation about it with them first."

"Perfect. Now, tell me more about everything that's been going on with you. Tell me about the travels, the writing, how things have been going between you and Jemma..." Lia took a sip of her wine and leaned forward in her chair. "Don't leave anything out."

Isabella put the forkful of pasta down that she'd been about to put in her mouth and leaned forward in her own chair, the big grin back on her face and the comfortableness between them as easy as if they'd known one another for a lifetime and not the mere months that it had been.

Lia loved this time with Isabella. Yes, she'd been blessed—beyond anything she'd ever deserved, in her own opinion. Sitting there across from her granddaughter, who looked every bit like Arianna, brought back a rush of memories and just a hint of sadness. But Lia had made peace with the mistakes of her youth a long time ago. Now it was only about cherishing the times that she had with those she loved and creating new memories.

TWO

Gigi loved shopping at the market in Castellina in Chianti whenever she was visiting Lia and Antonio. Today she was in charge of picking up the ingredients for the upcoming Christmas dinner that Lia and Chase would be preparing. This alone was enough to make her feel entirely useful and happy, but today was extra special because Isabella had come along to help her.

She smiled as she heard Isabella's decent attempt in Italian to request the cheeses that Gigi had sent her in search of. It was wonderful to see how confident and comfortable the young girl seemed. She looked like she belonged there—in Italy.

She walked up to where Isabella stood waiting for her change.

"Did you find everything, honey?"

"I think so, yes. Oh, did you see all those gorgeous flowers on the other side? I wanna get some for the bedrooms."

"You have a knack for beauty, Bella." Gigi flashed on a quick memory of Arianna rushing into the Sausalito house with arms full of flowers and requests from Gigi to put them everywhere throughout the house. "Just like your mother," she added.

"Do I?" Isabella turned toward her, always seemingly ready to have a conversation about her birth mother. "I feel like Arianna was such a fashionista—something I'm so obviously not—I've never really thought about the fact that I do like to make things beautiful, though." She grinned and gave Gigi a quick hug. "Thank you for saying that."

Gigi laughed. "Bella, you're such a sweetheart. It makes me so happy to spend time with you."

Isabella looked at her for a few seconds, then leaned over to kiss her cheek. "I love spending time with you too. And on that note, shall we get a coffee before we go home? We can pick one up on our way out and go sit in the square."

"That sounds like a great idea. I think we've got everything we need. We'll stop by the butcher on the way back to place our order—strict orders from Lia to get it in early, so she can be sure to get the best cuts of the meats she wants."

"Ooh, my mouth is watering just thinking about the feast they're going to prepare for Christmas dinner."

Gigi nodded. "I know. Me too. Douglas and I have been looking forward to this time for weeks."

"Do you miss him?"

"Yes, honey. I always miss him when we're apart. It's hard to imagine I lived so many years without him." Gigi laughed and noticed a look on Isabella's face. "What's that look I'm seeing?"

"Oh, I don't know. I just really love being around such happy couples—especially during the holidays—and I hope I can find that one day, you know?"

"And why wouldn't you?"

"Well, so far I've not been so lucky in that department."

Isabella laughed, but Gigi could sense something going on with her.

She'd noticed a quietness about Isabella since she and Jemma had arrived. In the back of her mind, she wondered if it had to do with the fact that Thomas had decided to stay back in London, but Gigi didn't want to pry, especially when Isabella had been so open with her during their time in San Francisco together. No matter how it might look, Isabella and Thomas were only best friends. That's what she had said when Gigi had asked about their relationship.

Gigi turned toward Isabella now as they sat on the bench in the square with their espressos in hand. "Bella, you're so young. You're sure to find love—if that's what you're talking about. Love will find you. Take it from someone who knows."

Isabella laughed. "When I least expect it, I suppose. Isn't that how the saying goes?"

"That's right, my dear." Gigi smiled. "Speaking of—do you want in on a little surprise?"

"Of course."

"Well, Douglas is bringing a guest with him—someone that I hope Jemma is going to be very happy to see." Gigi laughed. She had talked to Douglas about the possibility of Jemma wanting a heads up, but Douglas had insisted that she'd be happy about it—that she and Rafael had kept in touch over the past months and Rafael really wanted to surprise her with his arrival.

Isabella's eyes were wide. "Is it Rafael?"

"Ah, so Jemma has talked about him to you. Very interesting."

Isabella laughed. "She has. Yes. She told me about how good a friend he'd become since she stayed with you at the orphanage

—well, Jemma told me all about that time. And I've met him on video chat. He seems sweet."

"He really is. I hope she'll be happy to see him."

"I think she will be."

Gigi saw a look pass over Isabella's face.

"What is it, sweetie? Are you okay?"

"What? Yes, I'm fine. Maybe just a little tired, I guess. But I'll have a rest when we get back. Right now I want to hear all about you and the kids. You know, Jemma and I were talking about a possible visit sometime soon. She's dying for me to see the orphanage and everything that you've both told me so much about."

"We'd love to have you, that's for sure." Gigi grew silent for several seconds.

"What is it? I know that look." Isabella smiled at her. "Is everything okay? With the orphanage? With you and Douglas?"

"Oh yes. Everything's good. I probably shouldn't talk about it yet, but—"

"But? Go on. I promise your secrets are safe with me." Isabella laughed.

"Oh, I know, honey. Douglas and I have been talking lately —about Casa de los Niños, our future plans. We're not getting any younger, you know. And it's important that we think about the future of the orphanage—for the sake of the children."

"Well, first of all, you and Douglas are the most active retired people I know. It's hard to imagine you two slowing down any time soon. But what are you thinking?"

"We've talked about moving here, actually—to Italy." Gigi felt lighter just speaking the words. She wanted the move. It was something that was feeling more and more right to her. "You know we have Tori there—she's been there longer than we have and she's more than capable of taking over. And she's ready for the challenge of it, I think. And it's not like we'd just disappear or anything. It's really more about the day-to-day running of things. Tori can handle all that and we'd visit for good long periods of time, of course."

Isabella was looking at her with a big grin on her face. "And you've mentioned all of this to Lia, I assume?"

"Of course, and your grandmother is fully on board—ever supportive and gracious with her invitation to us to stay at the villa for as long as we like."

"I'll bet. Well, I think it's a fantastic idea—one that I fully support." Isabella grinned and reached over to give Gigi a hug.

"Good. I'm glad you think so. Douglas and I are still having conversations about it. You know, the two of us tried being retired before and it didn't work so well." Gigi laughed at the look on Isabella's face. "Oh, nothing bad happened, we just found ourselves a bit bored with it all."

"Well, if you move here—near Lia—I'm pretty sure you won't be bored." Isabella winked at her.

"I love being here—helping Lia with the cooking." Gigi laughed. "You have no idea how far I've come in that department. Douglas loves it that every time we go home, I've learned a new recipe or two—not that it's easy to find such lovely ingredients in Guatemala. It's not—not out near the orphanage anyway."

"So if you moved here, you'd get a nice big villa with your very own huge kitchen again? Or Lia would just talk you guys into moving into one of the guest houses." Isabella laughed. "I think it sounds perfect."

Gigi put her arm around Isabella's neck, bringing her in for a tight squeeze. "Me too, Bella."

And in that moment, as Gigi looked at Isabella's smile and that twinkle in her eye that reminded her so much of Arianna, she couldn't imagine anything more perfect than being able to spend more moments like that in this place that she'd grown to love so much.

THREE

Blu waited outside the villa in the convertible that she and Chase had rented. She had a meeting in Florence at eleven o'clock, and Jemma and Isabella had said they'd wanted to tag along for the ride through the Tuscan countryside. She beeped the horn lightly, laughing, as the two young women came running out the front door.

"Sorry, Mom. My fault—all my fault." Jemma threw her purse in the backseat. "Bella, go ahead. You take the front on the way there and I'll have it on the way back."

Isabella looked back toward her friend and smiled as she opened the front door. "Don't listen to her. It was me. I was on the phone with Douglas. Sorry, Blu," she said.

Blu reached over to put her hand on Isabella's arm. "We're fine for time. Don't be sorry. Are you sure you two don't want to stay here?"

"Mom, no. We want you to drop us at the shop you were telling us about—the one owned by your designer friend. I'm making Isabella buy something cool—at least some new shoes."

Blu laughed at the look Isabella shot Jemma.

"What? You know it's true, Bella. You haven't bought new clothes in a long time."

"What are you talking about? I have the new dress we got in London."

"Okay. Good point. But you have been borrowing a lot of my clothes lately." Jemma laughed.

"Which I'm sure you encourage," Blu chimed in.

She'd enjoyed watching the two girls interact since she'd arrived at the villa the night before. It was apparent to everyone that they'd become the best of friends, and nothing could make Blu happier. It was like watching an updated version of all the memories she had of herself and Arianna when they'd been about the same age in San Francisco.

She glanced at Isabella beside her as she drove the car down the long driveway. "So did Douglas manage to get the tickets sorted out for you?" Isabella had made the announcement the night before at dinner that Lucas—along with his family—was going to be joining them for Christmas.

"He did. Can you believe it? They're arriving on Monday. I really can't wait for you all to meet them. I think the girls will really love Annie."

"Wait—Mom, did you know Lucas? From when he and Ari dated?" Jemma asked.

"No, that was a few years before I met Ari."

"Did Arianna—did my mother ever tell you about Lucas?"

Blu didn't answer Isabella right away. The truth that Arianna had talked to her just a bit about Lucas, but she wasn't sure if she should relay the extent of the conversation to Isabella. She wasn't even sure if she remembered it exactly right.

"It's okay. You don't have to tell me if you don't want to, but I wish you would. I can pretty much handle anything now."

"True," Jemma said from the backseat.

"But, I mean Lucas already told me that he didn't think that Arianna had loved him as much as he loved her, so it's not like I'm disillusioned about what their relationship was or anything," said Isabella.

Blu smiled at Isabella. She didn't need to keep anything from her. She'd already decided months ago that Arianna's daughter deserved to know anything and everything that Blu and any of the others could tell her about her birth mother. "Oh, it's nothing really bad, honey. I'd asked a few questions about him at different times when Ari had opened up to me about you and that time in her life—which wasn't often, by the way. She'd really only said that Lucas was a bit much—that maybe he wanted more of a commitment from her than what she was willing to give him—at least at that time anyway. I think she felt a little stifled by your father—by Lucas. But she didn't say he wasn't a good guy or anything like that. I think she did have a lot of respect for him.

"Thanks." Isabella smiled over at her. "I kinda didn't really expect anything other than that. He is a good guy. I think you'll both like him and his wife very much."

"And your parents sure are being cool about it, aren't they?" Jemma asked.

"Yeah, they really are. They continue to amaze me by how well they've handled everything. It's been so great to see them and I wasn't sure how much I was going to talk to them about Lucas, but they knew I'd been to see him and how it all went. Well, it just came up naturally in the conversation and they said they'd love to meet them too."

"That's really great, Bella. It's a wonderful thing to all be together for the holidays. This is going to be a special Christmas for all of us. I know your grandparents sure are happy to have you all here, and I couldn't even begin to tell you how much I've been missing that one." Blu laughed and gestured toward Jemma in the backseat.

Jemma laughed. "Mom, I saw you a few weeks ago in London."

"Oh, I know. But it's not the same when we're traveling—staying in hotels."

"Well, we're pretty much all traveling now—to get to the villa, I mean," said Jemma.

"But it feels like home, doesn't it?" Blu said.

Isabella was grinning. "I sure think it does. After those suites that Lia and Antonio had built just for us?" She looked toward Jemma in the backseat, laughing. "Lia even let us pick out the colors for the rooms."

Blu laughed too. "I think maybe your grandmother is secretly trying to build a commune on the top of that lovely hill where they live."

Jemma giggled. "Hey, that's not a bad idea."

Blu debated for a moment whether it was a good time to bring up to Jemma what had been on her mind all morning. She looked at her daughter in the rearview mirror, long blond hair blowing, a big smile on her face and a lovely sweetness about her that Blu had almost lost a few years back.

Her heart ached sometimes for the love she had for Jemma and Kylie. They'd been through some rough patches for sure, but with Chase by her side, she'd never lost sight of what had been the most important thing—family. It was something she desperately wanted for Jemma one day, and it was nice to see that her daughter had softened a bit—no, she'd softened up a lot in the last year or so. It was something Blu was keenly aware of, and it made her proud to think of how far Jemma had come.

"Hello? Earth to Mom." Jemma was laughing and tugging on a strand of Blu's hair.

"Oh, sorry, what were you saying?"

"I was just asking you about your meeting today? What it's for?"

"Well, funny you should ask. In fact, it's something that I wanted to talk to you about."

She noticed the look that passed between the two girls. "It's not bad, and it's just something we're thinking about—Chase and I."

"Okay. Go on. It sounds important."

"So this is very early stages, but we're considering a move to Florence."

"Really? Where did that come from? Wait, are you going to sell the beach house?"

"No, honey. We won't ever sell the house. Too many memories there, right?" She glanced again in the rearview mirror and then back at Jemma with a smile.

"Well, it's your house of course, but I love that house. Bella, you really need to go there some time, doesn't she, Mom?"

"Yes, Chase and I were actually just talking about how we need to do a holiday at our place before we move. It would be fun to have everyone to the beach."

"Okay, so what's this Florence move all about? Sounds rather exciting," said Jemma.

"It is. Chase has been offered a head chef position there at one of the best restaurants in the city. And me?—well, you know how much I love the fashion scene of Italy, and I've been doing so many European shows lately. It's still early stages, but one of my friends is introducing me to a real estate agent today. Chase will spend a few days at the restaurant before we fly home. And we'll see how it all goes."

"Wow. That sounds exciting, if you ask me," said Isabella.

Blu could see Jemma nodding in the rearview mirror. "I agree. As long as we're—as long as you're keeping the beach house—I'm on board."

Blu laughed at her daughter's words. "Well, I'm glad I have your permission then."

"Oh, Mom. That's not what I meant. You know I want you, Chase, and Kylie to be happy, and I do love Italy as much as we all seem to."

"I know, sweetie. I'm just teasing you. And you'll always have a room to come home to whether we're at the beach or somewhere else." Blu glanced over at Isabella. "As will you, my dear."

Blu certainly had come a long way over the years when it came to opening herself up to family and love—Arianna had taught her a lot about that—unfortunately, mostly after she was gone. And then Chase came along and broke right through any of the tough walls she'd still had up. There wasn't anything that was more important to Blu than her family.

She looked over at Isabella's striking profile in the front seat next to her and smiled. Arianna would always be a part of their lives, just as Isabella was now too.

FOUR

Jemma's favorite place to paint was outside on the terrace at Lia's and Antonio's villa. She loved how the early morning sun lit up the vineyard below, which went on for as far as she could see. Being here reminded her of how far she'd come in only a few short months.

It was hard to believe that not even a year ago she could have lost her life because of some stupid decisions with a guy who'd been so wrong for her. She felt like a completely different person now—someone with a love for life, her painting, her family, and her friends. The past months traveling with Isabella had been the perfect thing for her and it was getting to be time to decide what would be next.

She'd been talking to Gigi and Douglas about going to the orphanage again. She wanted to do some painting there—to paint some portraits of the children and capture everything she loved about Casa de los Niños. And she was also curious about Rafael. They'd been communicating sporadically the past few months; she'd always consider him one of her good friends, but lately their friendship seemed to be hinting at something deeper. She wondered if she was ready to take a chance—to explore where her heart seemed to be tugging her.

She'd only shared her feelings with Isabella, thinking maybe it would be the right time for her also to visit the orphanage. But Jemma didn't think Isabella was doing as well as she let on. The kiss that had happened between her and Thomas had really thrown her before they'd left London. She said that she was doing fine, but Jemma knew better.

"Hey, early bird."

Jemma looked up to see Isabella making her way across the terrace, a mug of what was sure to be lovely Italian coffee in each hand.

"Morning. I'll come join you at the table."

Isabella finished her painting with a final stroke of the most perfect color orange and headed over to join Isabella at the table.

"It's so gorgeous here, isn't it?" Isabella said.

"I think it must be the most beautiful place on earth. And can you believe what your grandparents have done since we've been here last?"

"I know. The place looks great, and I must say that we did an excellent job decorating our suites from afar." Isabella giggled. "Are we even crazy for thinking about leaving, Jem? Maybe we should just stay here for a few months."

"I know what you mean. I was just thinking about that, actually."

"About staying?" Isabella took a sip of her coffee and sat back in her chair.

"No, not exactly. Just thinking about our next adventure. Well, honestly I was thinking more about going to Guatemala. I guess I'll talk to Gigi and Douglas more about it this week. I think he's arriving any minute, yes?"

Douglas had gotten into Florence the night before. Gigi had told them that he was going to spend the night, and knowing him and his jet lag, he'd be up at the crack of dawn to drive to the villa.

"Mm-hm."

"What?" Jemma thought she noticed a look about Isabella.

"Huh?"

"You look funny." Jemma laughed.

"Gee, thanks. Nothing. I was just thinking about something."

"And?"

"Oh, just how great Christmas is gonna be this year—how nice it will be when everyone's here."

"Oh, I know. You have no idea how fun it is to hang out with Kylie here. She can't get enough of playing with Gabriela, and soon your sister will be here too. It's really pretty incredible how that all worked out."

"I know. I'm still pinching myself about Lucas coming. It is very surreal."

"Do you really think your parents are okay with everything? I mean, are you nervous about them meeting?"

"No, not really. I guess it might be a tiny bit awkward at first, but they've handled everything so well. I don't think this will be different. My mom's already gone a little bit crazy buying Christmas presents for the kids, Annie included in that." Isabella laughed.

"And they arrive the day after tomorrow?"

"Yep. Monday. And they'll stay the rest of the week."

This time Jemma knew there was something that Isabella wasn't saying. "Hey, are you okay?"

"Yeah, why?"

"I dunno. You just seem a little down, I guess. I know I promised I wasn't going to talk about Thomas, but don't think I've not noticed that you haven't been taking his calls."

"How do you know that?"

Isabella didn't look shocked exactly but Jemma guessed that she still didn't want to talk about Thomas.

"He texted me."

"Did he? And?"

"And he wanted to know how you were doing."

"So, what did you tell him?"

"I told him that you were fine. Busy. And that he should call you."

"And that's when he told you that I wasn't taking his calls?"

Isabella looked like she was trying to keep from crying, and Jemma didn't want to make her feel bad. She hated how upset the whole thing had made her friend feel. It really was a bit of a mess. She felt confident that the two of them would recover from it all, but not if Isabella wasn't speaking to him.

"Yeah, well, all I'm saying is that maybe you should talk to him. I guess I don't really understand why you're not. It seems like you left on good terms and all."

"I know. You're right. Honestly, I've just felt that I needed a little space from him—time to get my head around the whole thing, I suppose. Does that make sense?"

"Yes. Of course it does." Jemma noticed a car pulling up the driveway. "Hey, do you think that's Douglas already?"

Isabella grinned and stood up. "Oh, do you think maybe we should change out of our PJs?"

There was that look again. "Nah, we're fine."

Isabella came around and started smoothing Jemma's hair back.

"What are you doing?" Jemma laughed. "Trust me. Douglas does not care what we look like."

"Oh, I know. I'm just fixing your bed-head a little bit." Isabella giggled.

The two girls got up to walk over to the car just as Douglas got out.

"Well, aren't you two a wonderful early morning sight?" Douglas smiled widely as he put an arm around each of the girls.

"Surprise!"

Jemma heard the second voice from the other side of the car and rushed out of Douglas's arms into those of her friend's. "Rafael! What are you doing here?"

He squeezed her tight for several seconds before creating just a bit of space between them as he looked into her eyes. "Are you surprised?"

"I'm *so* surprised. Are you kidding me?" Jemma looked over at Isabella, still standing next to Douglas with a big grin on her face. "And you! You knew, didn't you?"

Isabella nodded and walked over toward the two. "Yep. I sure did." She stuck out her hand toward Rafael. "Good to meet you, Rafael. I'm Isabella."

"The lovely Bella I've heard so much about." Rafael grinned, bypassing her hand as he gave her a big hug. "I'm a hugger, Bella."

"Oh, we're all huggers around here." Douglas laughed as he saw Gigi coming from the house toward him. "Speaking of which—excuse me while I go grab that beautiful wife of mine."

Jemma looked at Isabella, and they both grinned at the happy reunion taking place between Gigi and Douglas.

"Let's give those two a moment, shall we?" Jemma said,

taking Rafael by the hand. "Come on in the house. I'll get you a coffee." She turned back toward Isabella. "Coming, Bella?"

"I think I'm gonna go for a little walk. I won't be long."

"Are you sure? Do you want me to come with you?"

Isabella was smiling at her, but Jemma wondered if she needed to talk.

"No. No, you go get Rafael settled. I'll be fine. Nice surprise, huh?"

Jemma knew how wide her grin was, and she felt her face was flushed with all the excitement as she took a few steps to give Isabella a big hug. "Yeah, I had no idea. I can't believe he's actually here."

Isabella was smiling at her. "Go. We'll talk later."

"Okay. Have a nice walk, Bella."

FIVE

Isabella pulled her jacket a little tighter around her as she made her way down the long driveway. The air felt cool against her cheeks, but she enjoyed it. Normally, she liked to walk at this time in the early morning. It usually helped her to sort out ideas she was having about her characters and what they were doing in her story. Today, she just needed some time alone to think.

She'd done everything she could to put what had happened between herself and Thomas out of her mind, but she was only lying to herself and apparently everyone else could see it too. She closed her eyes for a few seconds as she stopped at the bottom of the hill to stretch, breathing in the cool morning air as she did so.

She allowed herself to remember that one incredible moment that they'd shared in London—the kiss that had made time stand still for her. The kiss that she'd first thought might change everything. Had it really happened not even a week ago? She shook her head, as if doing so could make the memory go away. It was bittersweet to remember. It hadn't changed things —not for the better anyway.

Thomas was still with Natasha, still choosing her, and when Isabella was being totally honest with her feelings, it left her feeling hurt and angry. She knew that it was risky—maybe too risky, in fact—to take a chance that there was anything more than friendship between them. She'd told Thomas that she didn't want to risk it—what they had—but it was a lie. She'd risk it all to taste his kiss on her lips again—to not have to wonder if there was something more between them, maybe even the true love of a soulmate that Jemma had talked to her about.

But what could she do? She hadn't been taking Thomas's calls because she didn't trust herself to keep up the lie. And her greatest fear was that once words were spoken—her true feelings made known to Thomas—there'd be no going back. He'd feel awkward for not being able to give her more than friendship, and then there was Natasha, of course. No, she couldn't ever tell him. And she couldn't speak with him until she trusted herself to act normal with him.

She took her phone out of her pocket to check the time. She didn't need to go for a long walk. She needed to get back to the house, around her friends and family. If anything would help her take her mind of Thomas, it was the festivities happening around the villa these days, especially now that Rafael had arrived.

She smiled to herself as she remembered the look she'd seen on Jemma's face when Rafael had hugged her to him. There was most definitely something between those two other than just friendship. Isabella was sure of that after seeing them together. She was anxious to get to know him a little better; and knowing Jemma, she'd be wanting the three of them to spend some time together for the same reason.

She took one last deep breath in as she stretched her arms high overhead and then turned to go back up the long driveway to the villa.

Isabella laughed as she poked her head into the kitchen, where there seemed to be a lot of commotion going on. "What's going on in here and what smells so divine?"

Gigi came over to kiss her on the cheek and hand her a fresh scone wrapped in a napkin. "I just took these out of the oven. Go sit over there by the kids and I'll bring you a coffee."

"And they're delicious!" said Rafael right before he took a big bite.

Jemma was sitting on one side of Rafael—no longer in her pajamas, Isabella noticed—and Gabriela sat on the other side, staring at him like she couldn't quite figure out what was going on. She'd been adopted from Casa de los Niños when she was very young, so it was doubtful that she had any real memory of Rafael.

Isabella pulled up a chair next to the young girl. "Gabriela, do you remember Rafael?"

Gabriela shook her head, just as Lia entered the kitchen, bending down first to kiss Gabriela on the top of the head and then to give Isabella a quick hug.

"But she's seen lots of pictures of Rafael. Many of which are him holding her, isn't that right, Gabby?" Lia said.

Gabriela nodded and then reached out to hug Rafael, whispering in his ear just loud enough for everyone to hear. "I think I remember playing with you."

"And you're so big now. Are you really nine?" Rafael said, winking at Jemma next to him.

"Yes, I'm almost ten and so is Kylie." Gabriela's eyes were wide.

"Speaking of, where is that munchkin sister of mine?" said Jemma.

"Kylie's upstairs getting ready for our tea party. Oh—" Gabriela jumped up from her chair suddenly, as if she'd just remembered something very important. "I was sent here on a mission, actually." She grinned and looked at Gigi, who was already laughing at her.

"Would that mission have to do with getting some scones for your tea party?"

"You got it!" Gabriela gave Gigi a hug around the waist and then carefully took the small plate of scones that she handed her. "See you all later."

Rafael looked at Lia, who'd sat down in the chair that Gabriela had vacated. "She certainly seems like a happy child."

"She is. She's the best, and especially happy when all her friends and family are around. She and Kylie are pretty inseparable when they're visiting." She turned toward Isabella. "And just so you know, those two have big plans for when Annie arrives. They're so cute up there, making sure they have just enough chairs and place settings."

Isabella laughed. "I'm sure they'll be the best welcoming committee for a little girl who is pretty excited herself. I introduced them all to one another on a video chat yesterday. Gabriela was trying to give Annie a mini-lesson in Italian."

Lia reached out to take Isabella's hand. "Well, I can't wait to meet Lucas and the whole family."

"Do you have an idea when my parents are coming back?" Isabella asked.

Emily and Richard had left for Florence the day before,

promising they'd only be gone for a day or two at the most. Knowing her mom, Isabella guessed that she'd wanted to do a bit more Christmas shopping, which she knew would be fun for them in Italy.

"I think they're coming back sometime tomorrow. Well, your mom told me they'd be here in time for dinner."

"I'll bet." Isabella laughed. "They both love your cooking, and with both you and Chase in the kitchen, I don't think anyone is willing to miss a meal around here."

"Not me, anyway," said Jemma.

"Nor me," Douglas chimed in from the doorway where he'd been standing with his arm around Gigi. He walked over to give Lia a kiss on the cheek as she stood up from her chair. "Everything looks so wonderful, by the way. It always feels good to be here."

Isabella didn't miss the look that passed between Douglas and Gigi. She couldn't help but smile, as she thought about her earlier conversation with Gigi. It did feel as if they belonged there in Tuscany.

"Alright, gang, I'd like the older folks outside on the patio for a small meeting please," said Lia, as she grabbed for Gigi's hand. "Let's leave the kids alone so they can catch up."

Jemma laughed. "There are no quote unquote older folks in this house. Oh, and by the way, Mom and Chase went out early for a drive. Sorry. I forgot to tell you. And Chase said to let you know that he'll pick up everything you need for dinner."

"Perfect. Thanks, honey." Lia leaned over to give Jemma a quick hug before she went out to join the others on the terrace.

"I wonder what that's all about?" said Isabella.

"Oh, I don't think it's anything—just Lia giving us some privacy, I suppose," said Jemma.

Isabella didn't miss the fact that Rafael had Jemma's hand under the table and she was blushing in a way that Isabella had not seen before. There was something going on between the two, alright. Isabella felt herself grinning at Jemma, not wanting to embarrass her friend, but at the same time, unable to hold back her teasing.

"Maybe you two want a little privacy, I'm thinking."

"Don't be silly. Stay here with us." Jemma leaned over to swat gently at her arm just as Isabella's phone began to ring.

Isabella took her phone out to see that it was Thomas before zipping it back in her pocket.

"Bella." Jemma gave her a stern look. "Come on. Talk to him. It's been long enough."

Isabella felt her face grow warm as she got up from the table. "I will. Just not right now. I'm not ready to talk to him yet."

SIX

Isabella laughed as her mom showed her yet another outfit that she'd picked up for Annie in Florence. "Mom, good grief. That's a lot of Christmas presents."

Emily and Richard had come home earlier in the day with bags and bags of goodies from their shopping trip. It made Isabella truly happy to see them finally spending some money on the things that seemed to be bringing them joy. Although they weren't quick to accept extravagant gifts from Isabella since she'd gotten her inheritance, they had finally decided to take their retirement early and spend some of their hard-earned money on themselves. There was no need any longer for the money they'd worked tirelessly to save for Isabella's education. She'd finally convinced them of that.

"Oh, I know." Emily looked over at Isabella, her forehead creased as she held the dress up in front of her. "It's too much, isn't it? They're going to think I'm ridiculous. But look how adorable!"

Isabella leaned over on the bed to give her mother a long hug. "No. I'm joking. She'd going to love the presents—all the girls will—and I think it's incredibly sweet. You're incredibly sweet, Mom."

Isabella felt tears stinging her eyes for the love she had for her adoptive mother—the only mother she'd ever truly known. She deserved all the love and respect that Isabella had to give. Both she and Isabella's father had been so incredibly supportive throughout all the changes that had been happening in their daughter's life over the past months.

Emily looked at Isabella and reached out to wipe the tears from her face with one hand as she grabbed Isabella's hand with her other. "Honey—Izzy, why are you crying?"

"Oh, they're happy tears, Mom. I just really love you."

"Well, I love you too, sweet girl. And nothing makes your father and me happier than to be here with you—with everyone —right now. It's quite festive around here, isn't it?"

They both laughed when, just at that moment, they heard the Christmas music turned on downstairs.

"That it is. I think Lia and Gigi are definitely in their happy place with the house full of people."

Her mother was eyeing her with a look that Isabella recognized.

"What, Mom? What's that look for?"

"Oh, nothing. I've just been wanting to talk to you—about your trip, Harvard, Thomas..."

Isabella felt her face change. No one knew the history of her relationship with Thomas better than her mother and she hadn't told her much of what was really going on—she hadn't told her about the kiss. But her mother knew about Natasha.

"Well, the trip has been amazing. Traveling with Jemma was exactly the right choice. It turns out we make really good travel partners."

"And it seems you two have become the best of friends."

"Oh, we have. Mom, I really adore her."

"That's good, honey. And Thomas? Is everything alright between you two? Usually I'd have heard you mention his name at least several times by now, and you've hardly said one word about him."

Isabella looked away, unsure of how to answer. Maybe her mom could actually shed some light on everything for her. She did know Thomas better than anyone else in Isabella's life right now. She took a deep breath before she spoke.

"Something happened between Thomas and me—a kiss happened, actually. It was right before I left London. It was completely out of the blue and we both kinda freaked out about it afterward. And now—now I'm just not quite sure of how to feel."

Isabella couldn't help the tears. It felt good to open up to her mother and it felt good when Emily reached to hug Isabella to her.

"Wow, honey. I can't say that I was expecting you to tell me that."

Isabella leaned back so that she could look at her. "It's awful, right? A very bad idea that never should have happened."

"Now, I wouldn't say that. Wanna tell me about it? What's happened since then?"

Isabella nodded and filled Emily in on the conversation that she and Thomas had had, her confused thoughts about it all now, and the fact that she'd been unwilling to talk to him since the day they'd last spoken at the diner.

Her mother listened intently and finally, after there was nothing left to tell her, Isabella sat back and looked at her. "So what do you think? Is it hopeless? Our being friends again?"

"No. No, not at all. But I think you need to communicate with him. Don't you?"

"Yes. I know I do. I just don't trust myself, I guess."

"But Izzy, isn't that part of what these last few months have been about for you?"

"What do you mean?"

"Well, you've talked to your father and me so much about how you've been learning a lot about yourself and what it is you really want. You've been willing to take chances with travel and with your writing. So, maybe it's time that you start taking some chances with your heart, too? Trusting yourself, I mean— that you're going to be okay, regardless of the outcome."

Isabella sucked in her breath. It was surreal to hear her mom speaking words to her that felt so similar to the ones that her birth mother had written to her in a journal so many years ago. Dare she? She had only really shared the journal with Jemma that one time, but somehow this felt right to her.

"I think you're right. Thanks, Mom." Isabella leaned in to give her another hug. "I'll be right back. I want to share something with you."

She returned seconds later with Arianna's leather journal in her hand. She and Emily moved over to the sofa in the bedroom, reading the journal together, laughing and crying at the words that had been written so long ago from the one person who had brought them together as mother and daughter.

When they'd finished reading, Isabella studied her mother intently. "I hope that you're okay reading this. I mean, I'd never want to make you feel hurt or weird about anything."

Emily nodded. "I'm okay, sweetie. I'm glad that you've chosen to share this with me." She seemed to be studying Isabella's face for a few seconds while they were both quiet. "I think it's actually pretty incredible that Arianna did all this for you—all these letters, the map she left you. I think it's helped you a lot. Your father and I made some mistakes, that's for sure."

"No, Mom."

"It's okay, honey. We did. Somehow we didn't realize all the pressure that you'd been feeling—with the track team, how well you were always doing in school, the pressure you felt to get accepted to Harvard—"

"Mom, no. I don't blame you guys."

Emily reached out to take Isabella's hand. "I know you don't. I just want you to know—to *really* know—that's we've always been proud of you and that it didn't have to do with your grades or anything that you were aspiring to be or do. It's always been about the person you are, and we're as equally proud of you now as we've ever been, maybe even more so."

"Really?"

"Sure. It takes a lot of courage to do what you've done these past months. And mostly—well, mostly I'm just really proud of the young woman you're becoming."

Emily wiped at the tears that flowed freely down her cheeks and Isabella reached in to give her another big hug, before grinning at her.

"Even if I decide to not go to Harvard at all? Because I've been meaning to talk to you and Dad about that."

Emily laughed. "Have you now? And the answer is, yes. Even if you never set foot on any college campus in your lifetime."

"Well, good. Because I'm pretty sure that my future plans include more travel and lots of writing."

"Speaking of your writing..." Emily grinned at her daughter.

"We weren't, and I'll be filling you in about that soon." Isabella laughed and thought about all the presents she had yet to put under the tree. She knew that everyone would be surprised to see her book, and she could hardly wait to see their reactions.

Just as quickly her laugh faded as she thought about when she'd given Thomas's book to him. He'd reacted with the most amazing kiss that she'd ever experienced yet in her lifetime and it had messed her up completely. She sighed.

"Iz."

"Yeah, Mom?"

"Everything's going to be just fine. You'll see."

SEVEN

Jemma sat outside on the terrace with Gigi and Douglas, sipping her early morning coffee. She had such an appreciation for them—for everything they'd done for her, and most importantly for the way that they'd always loved her unconditionally. They were like the grandparents that she'd never had, and she knew that they felt the same way about her too.

Gigi reached over to squeeze her hand. "Honey, what did you think about your surprise yesterday?"

"About Raf?"

Gigi nodded, stealing a quick glance at Douglas. "Rafael wanted it to be a surprise, but I wasn't so sure it was a good idea."

Jemma laughed. "Well, I most certainly was surprised." She felt her face go warm. "And it was good. Really good."

"Sweetie, I don't want to pry—you know I don't, but he's quite taken with you, I think."

"Honey—" Douglas interrupted.

"Oh, shush. I'm not telling her anything she doesn't know," said Gigi.

"Oh, you two. Don't fight about me and Raf. And you know I think the world of him. Time will tell. Neither of us is in a hurry. We've got plenty of time, right?"

"That's right, honey. You take all the time you need. And if that includes you coming to Guatemala to spend some time with us all, all the better."

"Gigi." Douglas pretended to be stern, then he leaned over to kiss his wife squarely on the lips. "You leave them be. They'll figure it out."

"Oh, I know. I just want my girls to be happy."

"What girls?" Isabella said, walking out on the terrace. She leaned down to give Gigi a big kiss on the cheek.

"You and Jemma," Gigi said, putting her arm around Isabella's waist to pull her closer. "I just want to see you girls both happy."

"Well, I can't speak for Jemma, but I, for one, am pretty happy these days." Isabella laughed.

"Me too." Jemma put her hand up for a high five from Isabella. "Seriously, aside from any talk about guys, I'd say that the last few months have been pretty incredible for both of us, wouldn't you, Bella?"

"Most definitely. I've seen things and lived places I only would have imagined just a few short months ago. And Jemma has been the best travel partner I could ever ask for."

"Speaking of travel..." said Blu as she came out to join them at the table. "What are you two thinking might be next? Is anyone planning to come back to the beach? Because we sure would like to have you there."

Jemma looked at Isabella. They had yet to decide what their next location would be. Jemma was starting to feel her heart leading her down another path, and she wasn't at all sure that it was going to end up the same for Isabella. But she needed to talk to Isabella about that privately.

"We haven't really decided that yet, but we will. We need to —soon, I suppose."

Isabella nodded her head.

Jemma got up from the table. "And if you all will excuse me, I've promised Rafael I'd take him into town. Mom, is it still okay if I borrow the car?"

Blu reached into her jacket pocket and then handed Jemma the keys. "Yep, have fun."

"Are you going to Thyme? Lia's there and I'm sure she'd love to show him around," said Isabella.

"Yeah, I was planning on taking him for a little walk around town and then to the restaurant for lunch. Anyone want to join us? Bella?"

Isabella and Gigi looked at one another and laughed. "No. No," said Isabella. "You two go on. Lucas and his family are arriving this afternoon and I have a few things to do before they get here,"

"Oh, I didn't realize. I can stay. I'm so anxious to meet them."

Isabella stood up to give Jemma a hug. "Don't be silly. I'm sure you'll be back before they arrive and besides, I think someone is waiting for you."

Jemma followed Isabella's gaze to where Rafael was exiting the kitchen to come out to the patio. Wow, he looked handsome —in his dark jeans and white button-down shirt. They hadn't really had much time to spend alone together since he'd arrived, so she was looking forward to the afternoon. It seemed they had a few things to talk about.

Jemma felt herself smiling from ear to ear as Rafael came

beside her to take her hand and kiss her sweetly on the cheek before turning to everyone else seated at the table.

"Morning, everyone. It sure is lovely out here this time of day, isn't it?"

Gigi stood up to give Rafael a hug. "That it is for sure. Now, do you kids want some coffee before you go? Something to eat?"

Jemma looked at Rafael and then back at Gigi. "No, I think we're gonna get going. We'll pick up a coffee in the square. It will be a good way for Rafael to get a feel for the town."

Gigi leaned over to kiss Jemma on the cheek. "That's a great idea. You kids have fun."

"So what do you think?" Jemma turned toward Rafael seated beside her on the bench in the little town square that she loved so much. They'd stopped at one of her favorite cafes to pick up espressos and delicious-looking Italian pastries. The air was very crisp but the sun was shining. It was the kind of weather that Jemma had always really enjoyed, but she guessed that it was colder than what Rafael was expecting.

Rafael leaned down to kiss the tip of Jemma's nose. "Your nose is cold." He laughed and then seemed to be studying her face. "I think it's beautiful here and I think you're beautiful too."

Jemma's heart felt like it was beating a hundred times faster than normal. She and Rafael had grown close—first while she'd been in Guatemala that past year, and more recently as they'd been texting and talking more and more lately. But they had never officially crossed the boundary that existed between their friendship and anything more than friendship. They hadn't kissed yet.

She smiled up at him, wrapping her hands around her coffee to warm them up. She loved the look in Rafael's eyes. She didn't know how she'd ever left him before—he was the one who had cared for her, even when she'd continued to screw up while she was at the orphanage. His friendship had remained steadfast, and she'd never forget what it had meant to her during that rough time in her life.

Rafael took the coffee from her hands and set it down on the ground beside his own. Then he took both her hands inside his own, blowing on them to warm them up, all the while watching her face. "You're so cold. Is that better?"

Jemma could only nod and smile. She was sure he could hear her heart beating wildly and when he leaned forward, placing his hands on either side of her face, she felt sure that she was about to have a heart attack. He came closer still and again kissed first the tip of her nose, and then finally she felt his lips on hers, more gentle than she would have even thought possible.

Rafael leaned back and smiled at her. "Do you have any idea how long I've been wanting to do that?"

Jemma grinned and somehow willed herself to speak coherent words. "Well, I hope you liked it as much as I did, because I'd like for you to do that again." She laughed and leaned forward, meeting his lips with her own, and this time the kiss was longer and more intense. Jemma thought that it was by far the best kiss she'd ever experienced in her life and she knew in that instant that there was something incredibly right about kissing this boy—this man—beside her. Rafael had always made her feel safe and secure. He'd given her a reason to trust men after she didn't think that was ever going to be possible.

"What's that look?"

They'd finally stopped kissing and now Rafael was definitely studying her intently.

"I love kissing you, Jemma. It was worth the wait." He leaned in to give her another slow kiss, speaking while his lips were still close to her. "So worth the wait."

Jemma laughed. She felt like a schoolgirl—all giddy and in love. She'd have to keep her wits about her and not go too totally crazy over the things that were transpiring. But when she looked into Rafael's eyes, she knew there was no denying her true feelings. There was a time in her life when she wouldn't have dared to share her deepest feelings with a guy, but Rafael was unlike any of those other guys she'd ever dated. She knew that she could be honest with Rafael—that he deserved nothing but the truth from her ever, even it meant making herself incredibly vulnerable.

She leaned over and kissed him quickly on the lips. "Me too. Well worth the wait, I'd say for sure." She laughed. "Now, we could sit here on the bench and kiss all day, but I am starting to get a bit hungry. You?"

Rafael looked like he was deep in thought. "That's a tough one, actually. I almost think I could give up food for more kisses, but yes, I think I should feed you, my dear."

Jemma laughed and let Rafael pull her from the bench beside him for the single best hug she'd ever received.

EIGHT

Blu sat at the small breakfast table with Gigi and Isabella. Chase was cleaning up from the delicious salad he'd fixed for them and the girls were off in Gabriela's room playing.

"Isn't it just so nice to be here altogether?"

"It is," said Isabella. "And something I hope we'll all be doing a lot more of soon."

Blu caught the message behind the look that Isabella seemed to be trying to send her and laughed. "Gigi and I both are aware of one another's potential future plans—and including your grandmother, we all think it would be pretty incredible to live so close to one another again."

"Only then Bella and I will have to choose who we stay with when we come visit," Jemma said, walking into the room to come over and give Blu a hug.

"Oh, bite your tongue, daughter dear," said Blu, giving Jemma a playful swat on the behind.

"Nah, I'm betting we'll all pile back here when the young blood's in town." Isabella winked at Jemma.

"Speaking of..." Blu reached out to tug a strand of Jemma's hair. "Don't think I missed that little kiss Rafael just gave you before you came in here."

"Ooh, do tell." Isabella gave Jemma a big grin.

Blu laughed at the red that was quite apparent on her daughter's face all of a sudden, something that wasn't typical for calm and collected Jemma.

"Well, if you must know—"

"—And we must," Isabella interrupted, laughing.

"Rafael just kissed me for the first time—while we were sitting in the square."

Blu could see that her daughter was definitely blushing now, and she was delighted that Jemma was opening up to them about her romantic life. She'd been dying to know how things were going herself, but knew better than to try to intrude in her daughter's love life uninvited. That had never gone well in the past—but she had to remind herself that Jemma was practically a different person these days. She certainly had gone through a lot of positive changes over the past year. And somehow Blu instinctively knew that Jemma's decisions were the right ones— that she could be trusted to do the things that were right for her and the things that would bring her the most happiness.

Isabella practically squealed and jumped out of her seat to come around and hug Jemma. "Tell me every detail later."

Blu heard Isabella say this quietly in Jemma's ear, which made her smile. Whenever she looked at the two of them, she was reminded of herself and Arianna when they were the same age. It was so long ago, yet watching them in front of her brought back the memories as if it were only yesterday.

She reached out and brought Jemma's hair behind her

shoulder as she leaned in to kiss her daughter on the cheek. "Honey, you look very happy and Rafael seems like a really nice young man."

Blu and Jemma both turned toward Gigi in time to see her wipe a quick tear away from her eyes.

"Gigi, are you crying?" Jemma laughed. "Don't cry. Is the news that bad?"

"Oh, you. Stop teasing. You know how I feel about you and that boy. Douglas and I love Rafael as if he were our own son. We couldn't be prouder of the man he's become, and we also couldn't want a nicer young woman for him than yourself. So that settles it then—pretty much a perfect match in my book."

Everyone sitting around the table laughed, and Blu noticed Rafael and Douglas now out on the terrace with Chase, who'd disappeared from the kitchen shortly after the women had started chatting about kisses.

Jemma looked up and seemed to notice at the same time. "Oh, boy. I wonder if I should go out there."

"And save Rafael, you mean?" said Blu grinning.

Jemma laughed as she started to get up from her chair.

Isabella's phone rang from where she'd placed it on the table earlier just as Jemma was getting ready to walk away, and Blu didn't miss the eye contact between the two girls.

"Bella. Just take the call. Please."

Isabella was shaking her head. "No, I'm not ready." She pushed the phone toward Jemma. "You talk to him if you want."

Jemma picked up the phone and Blu heard her say hello as she walked away.

Blu caught Gigi's eye and shrugged.

Isabella seemed embarrassed as she turned toward Gigi. "What? I'm not ready to talk to Thomas. But I will be—soon."

Isabella had told the two women and Lia that she and Thomas were having a bit of a rough patch. Blu didn't know the details, but Jemma had shared with her that it was pretty serious. Now, Blu could guess by the look on Gigi's face that she was having a tough time holding her tongue.

"Honey, can I say something to you?" Gigi asked Isabella.

Isabella sighed. "Yes. Sure you can, and I'm sorry for snapping at you, Gigi."

"No apology necessary, and I do realize that this is none of my business, but I know how much this boy—this young man —means to you, Bella. Don't forget that I've seen the two of you together—and not so long ago, I might add."

Gigi had filled Blu in on how their time in San Francisco had gone over Thanksgiving, including Isabella's reaction to being at the house where Arianna had lived—and died—so many years ago. Blu could only imagine what it must have been like for Arianna to be in the house, and Gigi had said that having Thomas there seemed to make it that much more special for Isabella. And she'd told Blu that she thought there was something really incredible between Isabella and her best friend.

Blu didn't miss the tears that seemed right on the verge of falling as Isabella responded to Gigi.

"I know. You're right. But you don't know everything that happened, Gigi." Isabella looked down and then back at the two women. "Thomas—he hurt my feelings. And I just—I need a little time, that's all. I'm sure everything is going to be fine."

Gigi reached over to pull Isabella in for a hug. "I'm sure it will be, darling. I wanted to tell you that this—what looks like a

46

good old-fashioned stubborn streak—reminds me of your mom —of Arianna—when she was your age."

Isabella grinned. "Really? Was she that stubborn?"

"Oh, was she?" Blu laughed, memories rushing back all at once. "That girl was about the most stubborn person I've ever met in my life. Well—"

"—Until the end, you mean?" Gigi had a very serious look on her face and Blu knew instantly what she meant by her words.

"Yeah, that's what I was going to say. Arianna wasn't stubborn those last months of her life—not when it mattered most to her and to all of us, really." Blu reached over for Isabella's hand. "But can I tell you something about Arianna and her stubbornness?"

Isabella nodded.

"She regretted certain things. Oh, not at the very end— she'd worked through so much by that point—but throughout her life, she hadn't been great about letting people in, really. You're better at that, at your age, than Arianna was." Blu hoped that Isabella was getting the point of what she was trying to convey to her.

"About love? Is that what you mean?" Isabella asked.

"Yes, about love, I suppose." Blu hesitated and then laughed. "Although far be it for me to talk."

Gigi laughed also from across the table. "I was gonna say— before you met Chase, you were not so open to the idea of falling in love yourself."

"This is true." Blu winked at Isabella. "But my point is, don't let too much time go by before you fix things with Thomas. He sounds like a good friend—from what Jemma has told me, he's really pretty amazing and she says he adores you."

"And it *is* Christmas," Gigi chimed in, making Isabella smile.

"Yes, it is Christmas," Isabella said, smiling. "And I know you're probably right, so thanks for speaking up. I appreciate you both a lot." Isabella stood up to give first Gigi and then Blu a big hug, and then she walked outside to join the others on the terrace.

NINE

Gigi laid her head back against Douglas's chest as they swung back and forth on the glider swing, with a perfect view of Antonio's vineyard spread out before them that she never tired of, no matter how many times they'd visited now.

"It's so lovely here, isn't it, honey?" she murmured.

She felt Douglas's kiss on the top of her head and his arm tightening around her. "That it is—and quiet all of a sudden. Where's everyone gone to?" He laughed.

"Isabella, Antonio, Emily, and Richard have gone into town with Lucas and Kate—to show them around before it gets dark. I'm betting that Lia and Chase are in the kitchen cooking up some sort of scrumptious meal—which I should be joining them in shortly. And I think the others are probably still having a tea party with the kids." Gigi laughed. "Weren't the girls so sweet with Annie when she arrived? I just love hearing the laughter of the children around here."

"Mm-hm."

Gigi lifted her head so that she could look at her husband. "What's that? And I know that look." She laughed and poked him in the arm. "I know there's something on the tip of your tongue, so out with it."

Douglas pulled her back against him. "Well, I'm just thinking—about our plans with the orphanage."

"Yes."

"Honey, I just want to be sure that you're ready for it, when we decide to do it. You've gotten so used to having all your young ones around you. I figure it would be a big change leaving that behind, don't you agree?"

"Yes, I see your point. And I don't want to do it until the time feels right. But I love it here. Yes, I miss the kids at home but I know that they'd be in good hands with Tori. And of course, we'd visit all the time, right?"

"That's right. There's no reason that we couldn't."

"And besides, who knows? In a few years, if things keep going the way they're going with Rafael and Jemma..."

Douglas laughed. "Now don't be getting ahead of yourself. They only just shared their first kiss, didn't they?"

Gigi put her head up again to look Douglas in the eye. "Rafael told you?"

Douglas laughed. "He did. Yes. He was quite sweet about it, actually. Asking my advice and not wanting to rush things with our dear Jemma. But that young man genuinely loves her, I think. We can't get involved, Gigi, but I sure don't want either of them to get hurt."

Gigi nestled her face back against Douglas's chest. "I think they'll be married one day. I can just tell."

"Gigi!" Douglas laughed.

"Oh, I know, I know. I'm only telling you that."

"Good." He winked at her. "So, what do you think of Lucas? Does he seem different from the boy you remember so long ago? It must seem a bit odd to you now—seeing him after all these years and with his own family."

"I always liked Lucas. In truth, I'd wished that Ari and her parents would have been honest with him—about the pregnancy all those years ago. I think he really loved Ari and I always had the feeling that he would have stood by her through it all. But—well, of course it wasn't my place to say anything. You know how strict Ari's parents were. Once they'd decided how everything was going to play out, there was no looking back, and of course I needed to be discreet about it all."

"Which you always were. I know how much they appreciated that about you. They trusted you, not only with Ari while she was growing up, but really with everything."

"I know, but I do regret that Lucas didn't know. It wasn't right. It wasn't fair to him. I must admit that I've been feeling a little anxious about seeing him. I wouldn't blame him for having feelings about how we all sent him away from the house when he tried so many times to see Ari after everything had happened."

Douglas pulled Gigi in closer beside him. "Honey, I'm sure that Lucas forgives you, and hopefully the two of you will have a quiet moment to talk while he's here. If that's something that would make you feel better."

Gigi nodded. Douglas was right in that she probably would feel better once she and Lucas had a chance to talk. Regardless, it was all worth his coming anyway—to see Isabella's face when she saw Lucas.

When he'd first arrived, Gigi had seen Isabella tentatively look over at her parents—at Emily and Richard—who'd done nothing but smile and show their steadfast support for their daughter. Then Isabella had allowed herself to be swooped up into the big bear hug from the man who was her own flesh and blood. From everything Gigi had witnessed so far, Emily and Richard seemed at ease and welcoming as they met their daughter's birth father. It was really a wonderful thing to witness and something that Gigi really commended them for.

Douglas leaned down to tip Gigi's face up for a quick kiss on the lips. "I hear the troops arriving now. I think Antonio mentioned that he wanted to do some grilling for dinner tonight. I'm going to go see about giving him a hand." He reached his hand toward Gigi. "Coming?"

"You go on. I think I'll sit here just another minute. Tell Lia I'll be in the kitchen shortly to help her."

Gigi loved helping Lia and Chase in the kitchen. Tonight they were joined by Blu, Emily, and Kate, but Lia had finally convinced them to relax at the small table with some wine while she and Chase finished with the pasta course. The guys were out on the terrace grilling steaks, and Isabella and Jemma seemed to have the younger girls occupied with an intense game of Monopoly.

Kate watched intently as Gigi put more dough through the pasta machine.

"I gotta tell you, I really can't wait to taste this dinner. Isabella has raved about the meals that go on in this house, and if the smell is anything to go by, whatever you have going on in that pot smells divine."

Gigi laughed. "Now, I know Isabella wasn't bragging about my cooking, but these two...honestly, it's gonna knock your socks off."

Chase walked over to give Gigi a quick kiss on the cheek. "Oh, you hush now. You're the best student ever, Gigi—"

"—And you've come a long way, my darling," Lia finished.

"I suppose. I've had good teachers." She winked at Kate. "And also Douglas threatened divorce if I didn't learn how to cook him something besides scones and tea."

Everyone laughed. "Oh, stop. Douglas would think your bologna sandwiches were gourmet if you put a nice piece of cheese on them," said Blu.

"Meaning he's not so picky?" Gigi laughed. "Yeah, he's a keeper alright. And he certainly knew I couldn't cook when he married me."

Now it was Lia's turn to lean over and kiss Gigi on the cheek. "Yeah, but you can cook now. And that's a fact. Don't try to deny it. I'll let you cook at the restaurant when you move here. That's how much I believe in your abilities." She winked at her friend.

"Oh? Are you and Douglas moving?" Emily asked.

Lia cringed. "Sorry, Gigi. I guess that's really still very early stages. I shouldn't have said anything."

"Oh, I'm sorry," said Emily.

"No. No, don't be silly." Gigi walked across the room to join the women at the table. "It's still very early stages, yes. We don't have a date yet. It's just something we've been thinking about as a possible next step for us."

Gigi thought that Emily still looked embarrassed for asking the question and she reached out to put her hand on Emily's. "Believe me, you all will be the first people who will know about and be invited for the big move-in party. And it will be a celebration. The more Douglas and I visit, the more we fall in love with Italy and specifically Castellina. And with Lia and

Antonio here, it's really starting to feel like our lives could be here too."

"Well, I for one can certainly see why," said Kate. "After our tour today, Lucas and I think it's about the most charming place we've ever seen. It wouldn't take much to convince us." She laughed.

"Oh, be careful what you say around Lia," said Blu, and she and Gigi both laughed.

"Half of the buildings on this gorgeous property weren't even here last year at this time," said Gigi just as Lia came over to refill all of the women's wineglasses.

"Oh, stop. I am not going to apologize for wanting to be able to have my loved ones around me, and that"—Lia bent down to hug Kate—"includes you, Lucas, and that darling little Annie. You are always welcome. And I mean that."

"Thank you. You're so kind—you all are. I couldn't be more pleased about having Isabella in our lives—about you all. It really has been a huge welcome surprise all around."

Gigi raised her glass of wine. "To new friendships."

"—And may life continue to surprise us," Lia added as the women clinked their glasses together.

TEN

Lia came over behind Antonio, who was sitting on the sofa reading a book to four-year-old Annie. She put her arms around him from behind and leaned in to kiss him on the cheek.

"Hi, honey. What's that for?" Antonio turned his head slightly so that Lia could make out the smile that she loved so much.

She leaned down again and whispered in his ear. "I'm just so happy to have everyone here. Can you believe it? Our living room is literally filled with everyone we love right now."

Blu and Chase were sitting close by on the floor with the older girls playing a board game. Emily, Richard, Lucas, and Kate seemed fully engaged in conversation across the room on the other sofa and Isabella, Jemma, and Rafael were laughing at the nearby table.

Antonio grabbed her hand and brought it to his lips for a kiss. "Yes, I love it too. And I really love seeing you so happy."

"I think it's the perfect time to decorate the tree. Are you almost finished with your story?"

Annie looked up at her. "Two more pages left."

Lia laughed. "So, you've read this one before, then?"

"This is the third time tonight," said Antonio, a big smile on his face.

Lia winked, kissing him on the cheek again before she was off to the closet to pull out the ornaments for the tree. She and Gigi had decorated the house for Christmas long before everyone had started to arrive, but she'd left the tree to do all together, wanting to create a new tradition.

"Everyone, it's time to put the finishing touches on this magnificent tree that Antonio picked out for us."

Annie came running over to her. "Oh, do I get to help decorate your tree, Lia?"

"You do, sweetie. And this tree belongs to everyone—to our whole family."

Annie looked up at her with the sweetest expression on her face. "I love our family."

Lia felt tears sting her eyes. "Me too, honey." She looked in the box of ornaments until she found the one she was looking for. "Here's yours, Annie. Why don't you go first? Pick a spot and then we'll give these to your mom and dad."

Lia had found the most gorgeous handmade ornaments that a woman in town sold in a little shop; she'd had each person's name stitched on the ornament in beautiful crystals. She couldn't wait to see what the tree looked like all done up with them and with the twinkling white lights that matched what Antonio had put up outside throughout the vineyard.

Annie, Lucas, and Kate put their ornaments on the tree and Annie helped Lia to pass out the remaining ornaments. She'd picked up one for everyone, including Rafael.

She discreetly tucked Thomas's away in the box. She had a feeling that maybe he'd be there next year for his.

"Antonio, would you do the honors, please? And I think we're going to need the ladder for this one." She handed Antonio the angel for the top of the tree. "Isabella, I have one more for you."

Lia pulled out the last ornament as everyone stood around the tree, the girls oddly quiet as Lia took the final one out of the box and handed it to Isabella. It was the ornament with Arianna's name on it. Lia went to stand next to Antonio, putting her arms around him as they watched their granddaughter take a few steps up the ladder that Antonio had left out.

"I think Arianna's should go near the top—near the angel," said Isabella.

When she was finished, she came over to give both Lia and Antonio big hugs. "It's as if she's looking down on us—at this family she helped put together—isn't it?"

Lia didn't miss the tears in Isabella's eyes as she spoke. It was a touching moment and the room was silent. Even the children were quiet as Antonio strung the lights and the whole room was lit up by the tree.

Lia brought Isabella in for another tight hug. "I think Arianna is always looking down on us—proud to see us all here, spending time with one another, loving one another. She would have loved that so much, Bella."

Isabella smiled at her. "I love you so much. I'm so grateful for how easily you all have taken me and my family in—it's really all been a dream for me—better than I ever could have imagined."

"Sweetie, your grandfather and I feel the same way. You are our dream. You do know that, sweet girl, don't you?"

Isabella grinned and nodded. "I have a lot to be grateful for. Sometimes I forget that and let little things drag me down."

Lia could only guess that her granddaughter was referring to the issues she'd been having with Thomas. "Thomas, you mean?"

Isabella nodded and then grinned as she pulled her ringing phone out of her pocket. "Wow—speak of the devil."

Isabella held the phone up so that Lia could see Thomas's name on the screen. "I think I should take this."

"I think you should too." Lia smiled as Isabella walked away, and then she stood back arm-in-arm with her husband, surveying the room, now buzzing with chatter and the laughter of the children.

"Honey, I think this is going to be one of our best Christmases yet."

Antonio leaned down to kiss Lia on the lips. "I think you're right about that, my darling."

ELEVEN

Isabella listened as Thomas filled her ear, first with apologies and then question after question, wanting to know everything that was going on. She felt herself grinning at the sound of his voice despite how nervous she felt about talking to him. She couldn't not talk to Thomas. It wasn't possible to cut him from her life. She knew it listening to him now, missing him and wishing she could watch the way his eyes crinkled when he laughed and the smirk he got on his mouth when he teased her.

"Thomas."

"Yes?"

"I need to tell you something."

"Okay, go on. Man, Iz. I'm just glad you're speaking to me. Please don't ever ignore me like that again. It was driving me mad."

"Was it?" Isabella's voice sounded quiet even to her own ears. Thomas always said the right things to make her feel better, and she was counting on him to do so now.

"Yes, goofball. You had to know that your not speaking to me was going to make me just a little crazy." He laughed but

Isabella had the feeling that neither of them thought the conversation was very funny.

"I know. I'm sorry. I just needed a little time. That's what I wanted to tell you. That I'm sorry." She felt like she was stumbling over her words a bit and willed herself to be normal.

"Okay. And now? Are you angry with me, Iz? I know I screwed up. But I—I can't handle it when you don't speak to me."

"I know. I'm sorry. I really am. It was immature of me."

"Well, unless you're saying you were doing it to hurt me— which I'm really not sure if that is what you're saying—then it sounds like you were trying to do the best thing for yourself. You know, I'll always get behind that, Iz."

Isabella swallowed the huge lump that had suddenly formed in her throat. Thomas had always supported her. For as long as she could remember, he'd stuck up for her and wanted the best for her. She'd never doubted that. She'd never doubted him or their friendship. Until the kiss. She couldn't stop the thought. It was there. It was probably always going to be there and she'd just have to learn to ignore it. She sighed.

"Iz? What? Did I say something wrong?"

"No. Let's talk about what's going on there. Have you been to a lot of holiday parties? How's everything going with Natasha?"

She couldn't not ask about his girlfriend. That would mean that things weren't, in fact, normal between them.

Thomas was silent on the other end of the line for several seconds.

"Everything's okay—for the most part."

"Care to elaborate on that?"

"Not really. I'd rather talk about you. When I talked to

Jemma the other day, she told me that Lucas and the family were coming. How has that been? Okay with your parents there and everything?"

"Yes, it's all been so easy, really. It's remarkable how much everyone fits in here—or more likely it's just that Lia, Antonio —and everyone, really—are so very welcoming."

"It certainly sounds like it."

The phone went silent for a few seconds.

"Thomas? Still there?"

"Yep. I'm sorry everything got so messed up, Iz. I never meant to hurt you."

Isabella took a deep breath before she spoke. "I know. I know you didn't. I'll be okay. I just needed a little time. I need to figure out what I'm going to do after Christmas."

"What are you going to do?"

"I don't know. Jemma and I need to sit down and talk about it, but Rafael's here now so I'm not sure if that is changing things for her or what. I'm kind of assuming that it is, the way those two seem to be hitting it off." Isabella laughed.

She was incredibly happy for her friend and had to admit that it was hard to imagine her and Rafael not ending up together. He seemed pretty clear with his intentions, and from the few little conversations she'd had with Jemma since his arrival, she seemed to be doing a good job opening up to the possibility of real love with him.

"Who's Rafael?"

"Oh, sorry. It's a long story. I'll fill you in another time."

"Okay. Well, I suppose I should get going."

"Natasha is waiting for you?"

The phone went quiet again. Isabella got the distinct

impression that there was a lot that Thomas was not talking about.

"No. No, she's gone to her parents' place in the country."

"Oh?"

"Yeah, we had a bit of a falling out, I'm afraid."

"Well, are you going to fix it in the next few days? Before Christmas?"

No matter how annoyed Isabella felt toward Natasha, the idea of Thomas alone in London for Christmas was not going to make her feel any better.

"I don't know, Iz. We'll see what happens, I guess. We're talking today, anyway. But don't worry about me. You go be with your family. Give everyone my best. I'll phone you again on Christmas, okay?"

Isabella felt herself smiling. It felt good to be talking to Thomas again. It felt normal, and she realized that amid all the changes in her life, she was liking normal these days. "Yeah, that sounds good. Thanks for calling, Thomas."

"Izzy?"

Isabella looked up at the sound of her mother's voice to see her peeking in from the doorway.

"Oh, hey, come on in."

"Lia told me that you were in here on the phone with Thomas."

"Yeah, I just hung up with him."

"How'd it go? Do you want to talk about it?"

Isabella looked over at her mom and then wrapped her arms around her neck. "I'm so glad you're here, Mom."

Emily laughed. "Where else would we be, silly girl? I've missed you a lot, and it would be hard for your father and me to imagine not spending Christmas with you." Emily took Isabella by the hand and led her over to the small sofa in the corner of the room. "Now tell me about Thomas. Is everything okay now? I must admit to feeling a little anxious about the two of you."

"Really? How so?" Isabella was genuinely curious about what her mother was referring to.

"Oh, I know that friendships change—that they come and go—but I've always imagined that the two of you were sort of in it for the long haul, you know?"

Isabella smiled, remembering the conversation that she'd finally just had with her best friend. "Well, I think we are too. And the conversation actually went pretty well. At least we're talking again now."

"That's good, honey. You look like you're feeling better about things."

"I am. And tell me about you and Dad. What do you think about Lucas and Kate? Mom, everything seems great, but I really hope it hasn't been too awkward for you and Dad. You'd tell me if it was, wouldn't you?"

Emily seemed to be studying her. Isabella knew that she was probably carefully weighing her words, but at least nowadays Isabella felt confident that she and her mother were doing a great job communicating, something that wasn't always the case between them.

"I'm not going to say that we weren't nervous to meet Lucas—to see the two of you together. I'm sure that has to be a bit strange for your father. But honey, it's so worth it to see you happy and I can tell that meeting him—meeting all these new people in your life—has been life-changing for you. And your father and I could not ask for more than that for you."

Isabella hugged her mom as she felt overcome with

emotion. "Thanks, Mom. It means so much to me—your support. And I can't tell you how happy it makes me that you want to be a part of everything—of everyone here. And it means a lot to them too. Lia, Gigi, and Blu just think the world of you."

Emily looked her in the eyes. "Well, it certainly helps that everyone is so welcoming and lovely, and that includes Lucas and Kate. We've really enjoyed getting to know them, and your father and I think they are a very sweet family, including that little sister of yours." Emily laughed.

Isabella couldn't talk about Annie without grinning. "Annie's great, isn't she? I knew she wasn't shy, but it's wonderful to see how easily she fits in with the girls here. And they took her right in under their wing."

Emily laughed. "Yes, she told me yesterday that Gabriela invited her to live here with them."

Isabella laughed too, and they both turned toward the door when they heard Jemma's voice as she entered the room.

"Bella? Oh sorry, I didn't mean to disturb you two."

Emily stood up from the sofa. "No, come in. I need to go see if there's something I can help Lia with in the kitchen."

Emily gave Isabella a kiss and a hug, and Jemma came to sit beside Isabella on the sofa, handing her a mug."

"I come bearing gifts of hot chocolate in my quest for a much-needed chat with you."

Isabella laughed at the look on her friend's face and settled back into the sofa. With her long-awaited chat with Thomas and now the familiar feeling of settling into a good long talk with Jemma, it seemed that she was getting a bit of normalcy back in her life once again.

TWELVE

Jemma was dying to talk to Isabella. Firstly, about the conversation she assumed had happened between Isabella and Thomas, and secondly, they needed a good catch-up chat after everything that had happened between herself and Rafael. Jemma was still pinching herself over everything that had transpired in the last few days.

"How'd it go between you and Thomas? Sorry, I saw you leave earlier with your phone and assumed it was him calling. Did you two patch things up?"

"Yeah, I think so. I mean, it felt great to talk to him. I'm not sure what it would be like to see him, but I guess we'll have to cross that bridge when we come to it."

"Well, I'm glad to hear that you're speaking to him. I'm sure he is too." Jemma leaned in to give Isabella a hug.

"Enough about me and awkward relationships…" Isabella winked at her friend. "That was pretty sweet what Lia did with the ornaments, huh?"

"So sweet. I love it here so much. Don't you, Bella? It just feels so festive and…"

"—And you and your sweetie are in a little lovesick bubble," Isabella finished, laughing as she spoke. "And I love that, by the way."

"Is it really that obvious?" said Jemma, grinning as she asked the question.

"Mm-hm. Definitely that obvious. He adores you, Jem. And he's really a sweet guy."

"He is, isn't he?"

"Well, not that I've spent much time with him since he arrived, but from everything you've told me and what I have seen—and certainly from the way he looks at you."

"Oh yeah?"

"Yes. As if you hadn't noticed." Isabella laughed and poked Jemma gently in her side. "Whenever you're in the room, I don't think he notices anyone or anything else."

"It's funny. I've always felt something with Rafael. Well, when I first knew him, we were only kids, really—like you and Thomas, I suppose. But even then, I felt an attraction to him—a wanting to be near him..."

"And then, when you saw him last year, you realized how devastatingly handsome he'd become," Isabella finished.

"Exactly." Jemma laughed. "I still remember seeing him for the first time pulling up in the boat. And I was such a confused jerk back then. But he just hung in there, taking care of me, and he was always there when I needed someone to talk to. If I really think about it, I'd say that Rafael saved me from a pretty awful time back then."

Isabella reached out to hug Jemma to her, and she didn't miss the quick tears in her friend's eyes. Jemma had shared with her friend everything that had happened while she was at the orphanage the last time—including the horrible mistake that she'd made ever thinking she belonged anywhere near that creep, Eduardo. Jemma shivered as the memory of what Rafael had probably saved her from flashed through her mind.

"I still can't believe that happened to you, Jem. I'm so thankful Rafael was there for you."

"Me too. And apparently he's still here for me now, no matter how much I pushed him away."

"But you've been good for a long time now."

"Yes, we have. Aside from how sweet he is and how I'm currently falling for him"—she laughed at the look on Isabella's face—"And yes, I do feel like I'm falling pretty hard. There, I said it."

They both laughed.

"Aside from all that, I'm so incredibly proud of him—what he's done with the loan I gave him. He's made such a success of his construction company in a very short time. He told me just today that he's got plans in place for expanding and he's about ready to pay the loan off in full. I always knew he'd do well, but his success has even shocked Douglas, I think."

Isabella was looking at her with a funny expression on her face.

"What? What's that look?"

"I think that's so great. I can't help wondering what you're thinking. When it comes to you and Rafael, I mean? Can you see yourself going there—to Guatemala to be with him?"

Jemma grinned. "You know, I can hardly believe that I'm saying this, but I think I can, Bella. I mean, I guess I can't imagine not being with him—at least at this stage. Like maybe we need to give our relationship a real shot, ya know? And I'm not sure we can do that if we're not in the same place."

Isabella was nodding her head, but Jemma guessed that

there was still a lot to be said. She didn't want to disappoint her friend in regards to the traveling they'd been doing together, but they hadn't yet decided what would happen after Christmas one way or another, either.

"I hope that you wouldn't be upset about that—I mean because of course it means I wouldn't be traveling with you, unless you decide to come to Guatemala yourself—which of course I want you to do. And I know Gigi and Douglas would love to have you visit them at Casa de los Niños..." Jemma knew she was rambling but suddenly it was very important to her that whatever she decided to do, Bella came to a decision that made her happy as well.

Isabella reached out to touch her arm. "Stop. Don't you worry about me. I'll be fine. The truth is, I'm not sure what I'm going to do yet. I have thought about Guatemala. That is one of many places on Arianna's map, as you know—and yes, I'm still pretty determined to see that goal through—in my lifetime, anyway." She laughed and then cringed as she looked at Jemma and recognized her poor choice of words probably at the same time as Jemma did. "Well, I guess we don't know, do we? What a lifetime actually will end up being."

"No, we don't. It's something to learn from Arianna, for sure, isn't it?"

"About living more in the moment, you mean?" Isabella looked thoughtful as she asked the question.

"Yes, I've been thinking about it and Arianna a lot lately. I suppose because of the holidays and the memories that I do have of being with her at Christmas. And also because we're almost to the age that she was when she passed away. That's so incredible to think about, isn't it?"

"And it's a good reason for you to take a chance on love—

on Rafael." Isabella grinned. "I think it absolutely makes the most sense in the world, and I'm proud of you for not second-guessing it all." Isabella leaned in to give Jemma another quick hug.

"And maybe you with Thomas?"

Isabella's head jerked up and Jemma had to bite her tongue about what she really wanted to say. She'd promised her friend that she'd not be talking about possibilities of more than friendship with Thomas any more, but that didn't meant that she didn't one hundred percent believe that the two of them belonged together.

"Jem." Isabella looked slightly annoyed but like she was trying not to be.

"No, I just mean second chances with your friendship—the fact that you're talking to him again and trying to get things back to normal. That's all." Jemma grinned at her friend, willing her to believe the words she was speaking.

"Okay. If you say so. And yes, I do know what you mean. It's not a time for holding grudges, that's for sure. Life is way too short for that, and Thomas and I have way too much history to let our silly impulses get in the way of years of friendship. Don't worry. I'm sure we're going to be fine."

Jemma nodded. "I know you will be."

"And I'm going to figure out what I'll do next, so don't you worry about me. You need to do what feels right for you. I'll always support that. Really, I want you to know that. And who knows? I may end up joining you in Guatemala. Maybe I'll talk to Gigi and Douglas while we're all here to see what their thoughts are about it."

Jemma laughed. "Well, if you ask Gigi what she thinks

about you coming, she'll have Douglas booking you on a flight so fast, you won't know what happened."

Isabella laughed. "Good point. I will approach the subject with care. And on that note, shall we go see what everyone is up to?"

"We shall." Jemma stood and then hugged Isabella one more time before they walked out of the room. "Thanks, Bella."

"For?"

"For just being the best friend I've ever had," said Jemma.

THIRTEEN

Blu smiled as Kylie and Gabriela performed their dance routine for her in one corner of the restaurant. They were planning to perform it that night during dinner as an intermission event.

"Mom." Kylie was trying to get her attention, as Blu had apparently zoned out thinking about everything she had yet to do.

"Yes. Sorry. You were saying?"

"This is where Annie will be. Gigi is making her costume. She can't practice now because her mom said that she needed to take a nap, but we taught her the steps earlier and—Mom, she's so cute."

Blu got up to give her daughter a big hug. "Kylie, honey, I love that you are so kind to Annie." She turned toward Gabriela. "Both of you girls are going to make wonderful babysitters one day soon. You're naturals."

Kylie and Gabriela beamed with pride. They were good girls and Blu was always thoroughly entertained by the pair of them, as was everyone around them.

Tonight, Lia was having the annual Christmas party and

dinner at the restaurant. The whole crew from the villa would be there, as well as everyone who worked at Thyme and many of their regular local customers. Blu had been there during this time in past years and thought it was a very fun event. Lia pulled out all the stops in the kitchen and she'd invited Chase to help her cook. Blu was in charge of decorating the dining room; she'd wrangled Jemma and Isabella in on that to help her.

Jemma came up from behind Blu to put her arm around her with Isabella following close behind.

"Hi, honey. It's looking good so far, don't you think?"

"I do. All the garland makes it look very festive in here."

"Where's Rafael?"

"Oh, he went to help Douglas with something. I think maybe Lia asked them to try to find some emergency ingredient that she needed."

Jemma moved over around one of the bigger tables to help Isabella with the cutlery as Blu started folding the napkins at one end of the table.

Blu watched Isabella as she carefully organized each setting the way that Lia had shown her earlier. It was still alarming to Blu how much Isabella looked like Arianna. She tried not to spend too much time staring at her for fear of making her uncomfortable but it was moments like this—with Isabella so unaware of her own beauty—that caught Blu off guard.

It had never been like that with Ari. Ari was well aware of her beauty—not really in a snobby sort of way, but more in a matter-of-fact way. Isabella? Bella seemed to have no idea how naturally beautiful she was.

Blu came around beside Isabella, giving her a big hug.

Isabella hugged her back and laughed. "What's that for?"

"Yeah, Mom. Are you getting very sentimental today?"

Jemma teased her as she watched the two from the other side of the table.

"Yes. I suppose." Blu laughed too, but then she took both of Isabella's hands in her own. "I'm just really happy that you're here with us. It's a special Christmas, that's for sure."

Isabella grinned. "Thank you, Blu. It means a lot to me too. Meeting you all and becoming a part of your family has been one of the best things to ever happen to me." She winked at Jemma. "As well as meeting this one over here. Seriously, Jemma is one of my best friends—definitely the best girlfriend I've ever had for sure."

"Well, I'm sure that my mom will attest to the fact that you've also become one of my best friends. How we ever managed so many years without one another is beyond me." Jemma laughed, as did Isabella.

Jemma stopped what she was doing to look at Blu. "It must be strange for you, Mom—to see Bella at the same age as Ari was when you were friends. Does it make you sad?"

Blu didn't answer Jemma right away and she saw Isabella watching her carefully too.

"I wouldn't say that it makes me feel sad exactly—only because so much time has passed. But it does make me feel nostalgic for sure. It makes me think about Ari and what she would have been like with our dear Isabella." Blu smiled at Isabella. "She would have adored you and been so proud to have you for a daughter. I do know that much."

Isabella smiled back at her.

"And she would have absolutely loved the fact that the two of you have become such good friends. We all love that," said Blu, grinning.

Isabella looked thoughtful.

"Bella, what is it?"

"You know, it's weird. Sometimes I actually forget that I never knew Arianna. Between all the stories you've all told me, the pictures, and especially the journals that she left me, I feel as if she and I have actually spent time together. I don't know if that makes sense at all."

Blu smiled even wider. "Do you have any idea how happy those words make me? It was Ari's most important request of us before she passed away. She wanted you to have a sense of who she was. So, to hear you say that is really pretty spectacular."

Jemma came around the table to give her mom a hug. "Job well done!"

"Seriously. I can't ever thank you all enough for that," said Isabella. "When I'd found out my birth mother had passed away —that I'd never have the chance to know her—I was devastated at the loss I'd felt. I just never would have imagined that feeling of loss could be replaced by something as rich and wonderful as what you've all given me."

"Bella, I think the others would agree that we feel the same way about what having you in our lives has meant to us. Losing Arianna was one of the hardest things I've ever dealt with, but meeting you—knowing you—has brought back some of the joy that left us when she died. And we just love you so much, honey."

Blu hugged Isabella close, pulling Jemma in with them also.

"What a love fest." Jemma laughed.

"You bet it is." Blu laughed too, happy for the new memories they were creating and excited to see what the future would hold for them all.

FOURTEEN

Lia placed the last platter of food on the table and looked around at her guests. Every table was full, every chair occupied by someone who'd made a difference in her life. The main large table was filled with all her guests from the villa—her family. And Lia loved that this group was growing bigger every year.

At another table nearby sat her good friends, Rebecca and Marco. Lia smiled as she watched Marco trying to feed Rebecca a huge mouthful of pasta, her mind flashing back to the chance meeting on an airplane that had let to the reunion between her and Antonio. Looking back at everything that had happened, Lia no longer believed in chance encounters. It was fate that had brought her and Rebecca together that day, fate that had her sitting next to the wife of Antonio's dear cousin, Marco.

She walked over to greet Elena and Franco before she sat down. Lia had been a fish out of water—and a rather depressed one, at that—when she'd arrived in Italy all those years ago to make her first home in the quaint little guesthouse run by Elena and Franco. They'd been a godsend to her during that time.

Elena, gently coaxing her back to her love for cooking and where she belonged—in the restaurant with Carlo. She and Antonio had remained friends with the couple, who were regular visitors to both Thyme and their home at the vineyard.

Lia looked around to see Sofia half dragging her uncle, Carlo, from the kitchen to the table to eat. Lia laughed because she knew how happy Carlo always was to be invited back into the kitchen. After Arianna had bought the restaurant from him, he'd stayed on cooking for several years before finally retiring, but at least every few weeks he'd show up at the restaurant with his apron, and Lia was happy to have him at Thyme as both guest and cook when it pleased him.

Lia smiled at Antonio as he came to her side with a glass of champagne.

"Honey, do you want to do the honors?" He walked her to one side of the dining room where they stood together, Antonio's arm around her waist.

The room grew silent as all eyes looked toward their hosts, Lia so poised and lovely in the blue gown she'd purchased especially for the evening. She swallowed and told herself not to get too emotional. She had a few things she wanted to say and she needed to be able to get through her little speech without breaking down.

"Thank you all for coming. Antonio, I, Sofia, and everyone here at Thyme honors you as our friends and family. Your faces are the ones we can't wait to see at these tables every day throughout the year, and we want to thank you for continuing to let us serve you our favorite dishes week after week. It is because of you all that Thyme continues to be one of the favored restaurants in the area, and we couldn't do that without your support." Lia raised her glass, looking around the room at each person seated. "We wish you a Merry Christmas and the happiest New Year to come."

"*Buon appetito.*" Antonio raised his glass alongside Lia's.

After finishing their desserts, Blu and Gigi both moved around to the other side of the table to sit next to Lia. It had been a fabulous meal and now the guests were starting to get up from the tables to chat with one another. Lia had hired one of her favorite local musicians to play carols on the guitar quietly in the background. The children were playing near the Christmas tree in the corner, eager to finally have a chance to open the presents beneath it as soon as one of the grown-ups gave them the green light.

Lia turned toward her friends. "Well, how was it? Did you both get enough to eat?"

Blu laughed. "It was absolutely wonderful, as usual, and I can't even think about eating another bite."

"I know I say this every year, but every year you surprise us with the most wonderful new dishes," said Gigi.

"You're both sweet. Thank you. And this year, Chase is definitely responsible for a good portion of the menu. I'm really excited about that new opportunity he has in Florence. If he takes it, they'll be lucky to have him—as will Antonio and I—in regards to having you both so close." She reached out to grab Gigi's hand next to her. "And you! I think maybe we should seriously start talking about your future plans, missy."

Gigi laughed. "Yeah, somehow I'm not so sure that Douglas is taking me seriously about it all. Well, in his defense, he knows that we both stunk at the whole retirement thing years ago."

Lia laughed. "The key phrase there being years ago. You've

mellowed so much since then—and I think you and Douglas together have really hit a nice stride, haven't you?"

"We have, yes. We don't work nearly as hard as we used to. Of course the orphanage has become more of an emotional thing for us. Tori can run it. She practically is right now and she's great at it. But I will miss the children. That's for sure."

"Well, that certainly does sound like something that *is* happening, then." Blu grinned. "Won't it be nice to be able to see one another again whenever we like? I miss those times, and it's been a good long while now. Who knew that Italy would call us all to her like this?" Blu winked and the three women all grinned at the same time.

"I think we all know the answer to that question," said Lia.

Gigi nodded. "Arianna does seem to have a way of bringing us all together."

"Just like she wanted," said Blu quietly.

Lia looked at them both sitting beside her. "Isn't it pretty amazing?"

"What's that?" said Blu.

"I just count myself so blessed to have you both in my life. It's a miracle to me that I actually took the chance on contacting Arianna all those years ago when I did. To think what would have happened if I had waited." Lia's body visibly shook at the thought of it.

Gigi put her arm around her friend. "Well, it's a good thing that you don't have to think about those what ifs. Everything happened exactly how it was meant to happen. And let's not forget that it wasn't just good timing for you. It was a timing that made all the difference to Ari. I know that for a fact, as do you."

Lia and Blu nodded their heads in agreement with their friend and Lia wiped away a single tear—not of sadness, but gratefulness for everything and everyone that she had in her life.

FIFTEEN

Gigi smiled at Lucas when she saw him making his way across the room toward her table. Everyone seemed busy chatting, and the kids were amused by the gifts that Sofia had given them earlier in the evening.

Gigi had been feeling that a nice chat between her and Lucas would probably do a lot to put her mind at ease about one of the only regrets that still haunted her from time to time, so she welcomed him approaching her now.

"Gigi, can I get you a wine and then join you for a bit?"

"That sounds lovely, Lucas. Yes, please." Gigi handed him her empty wine glass and watched him walk over to the bar in the corner, stopping where his wife sat for just long enough to lean down and whisper in her ear. Gigi didn't miss the quick brush of their lips and the genuine happiness that seemed to radiate from him and Kate whenever she saw them together. She'd spent hardly any time yet with the pair, but it was evident to her that they were well suited to one another.

"Here you go." Lucas put her wine down on the table in front of her and then sat down opposite her at the small table.

"Thank you," said Gigi as she started to raise her glass to her mouth.

"To Tuscany—and to Isabella," Lucas said, holding his glass out beside hers.

"Cheers to that. Do you like the wine?" It was one of Gigi's favorites from Antonio's vineyard.

"I do, yes." Lucas was quiet for a moment. "Gigi, I just wanted you to know that I don't blame you—for anything in the past, I mean." He placed his hand over Gigi's and her eyes instantly filled with tears.

She took a deep breath in to try to calm her tears before she spoke. "I've thought about you a lot over the years—about the secrets, about Isabella—before we all met her, I mean. It feels like ages ago and then I have to remind myself that it's been only months now. As soon as she knew there was a chance of finding you, she wanted that. And I must admit, the relief I felt was so great, Lucas. I always wanted you to know that you had a daughter."

Gigi stopped to wipe her eyes on the napkin that she held in her hand.

"Please don't cry. I would hate for you to feel anything other than happiness now for how everything has turned out. We can't change the past—neither one of us. The important thing is that we've all come together now. The fact that Isabella is in my life is nothing short of a miracle to me—the fact that she even exists. Of course, it's unfortunate that I missed so much of her life—that we all did—but from the looks of things, I'd say that the future seems pretty bright."

Gigi smiled, feeling any anxiety she'd been holding onto about Lucas leave her body. He was the same gentle boy she remembered from so long ago.

"You were always so good to her, Lucas. Arianna knew that, even though I know she didn't always treat you the best when you were together."

Gigi used to scold Arianna tirelessly about how flippant she was in her relationship to Lucas; and then after she'd returned from being away to have Isabella, Arianna couldn't even be convinced to speak to him. Gigi knew that it had been mostly Arianna's own guilt along with the pressure of her parents, but it didn't excuse the confusion that Lucas must have felt at the time.

Lucas was shaking his head. "Arianna never felt for me the way that I felt for her. I knew that, even before she went away and everything ended. And well, there's nothing really to say about it now. I'd hate to think that Arianna died without forgiving herself; from what Isabella has shared with me, it seems that she had given herself the gift of forgiveness in the end. I'm grateful for that—and most of all, for the chance to know Isabella. That's all that matters now."

Gigi nodded. "And you have Kate and Annie, who both seem so lovely."

As if on cue, Annie come running from across the room to hurl her little body into Lucas's lap.

"Daddy! Look what Miss Sofia gave me." She held up a small doll with wavy blond hair and a beautiful woven gown. "She says she picked her out because she looked like me—from the picture that Bella showed her from when she visited my room and had a tea party with me and Thomas at our house in San Francisco." Annie stopped as if she'd just noticed Gigi sitting there across from her father. "Bella is my sister. She's real nice."

Gigi laughed. "Oh, I agree, honey. And she sure is happy to have you for a sister. And you know what?"

"What?" Annie's eyes were wide, as if she couldn't wait to hear a secret.

"We're all very happy that you came here to Italy to celebrate Christmas with us. I'm pretty sure that Santa got a special note to let him know that you were away on a trip."

Annie nodded her head. "Yes, Daddy helped me write a letter to Santa and we gave him the address of Lia's house." She scrunched up her forehead as if deep in thought.

"What's wrong?" said Lucas, winking at Gigi.

"Daddy, do you think Santa will be able to find the vineyard? It was an awful long drive from the airplane to get here. It was so long that I fell asleep, remember, Daddy?"

Lucas laughed and then adjusted his face when Annie looked at him so seriously.

"Oh, yes. Santa has helpers from all over the world that make maps for him of the different places. Santa never gets lost."

Annie jumped off Lucas's lap, all smiles again. "Okay, I gotta go tell Kylie this important information."

Gigi and Lucas looked at one another and burst out laughing.

"She sure is adorable," said Gigi. "And smart."

"She's a handful, alright."

Gigi followed Lucas's gaze to where Kate was laughing with the younger girls and waited for his attention before she spoke. "I'm glad things have worked out for you, Lucas. You seem to have a good life—a happy life. For what it's worth, in the end, I know that this is what Arianna wanted for you. She had really changed toward the end of her life." Gigi smiled at the look

Lucas gave her. "I loved that girl as if she were my own, but I know she was very selfish when she was younger—when the two of you dated." Gigi looked down at the table and then back up into Lucas's eyes. "But she did change in the end. She knew the mistakes she'd made and the wrongs that needed to be made right. She tried her best to make that happen."

Lucas reached out again to take Gigi's hand. "I can only imagine, and I'm so sorry for all the loss you've had. I hope that knowing now that I don't hold any grudges against you or Ari —against anyone—for that time will alleviate any of the guilt you've felt over the years." He squeezed her hand gently. "I really mean that, Gigi."

"Thank you, Lucas. You have no idea what that means to me."

Gigi felt something inside her shift. It was the final bit of guilt that she'd been hanging on to for all these years. Knowing that Lucas forgave her, and maybe more importantly, that he forgave Arianna, left her with a feeling of relief that she'd not even imagined possible. She quickly wiped her tears away as she saw Isabella coming toward them from across the room.

"Hey, you two." Isabella leaned down to kiss first Gigi and then Lucas on the cheek. "It's a nice party, isn't it? I think that Lia's meal was the best I've ever eaten, but she assures me that it only gets better with Christmas dinner at the villa." Isabella winked.

"You're right about that—which reminds me—I need to go speak to Lia about something. Sit here, Bella."

"Are you sure? I didn't mean to interrupt anything." Isabella looked from Gigi to Lucas, who'd gotten up to give Gigi a hug before she walked away.

"Yes. Yes, I'm sure." Gigi looked at Lucas after they'd

hugged. "Thank you, Lucas. You have no idea of the difference your words have made to me tonight. I'm extremely grateful and so very glad that you're here—we all are." Gigi looked at Isabella and then back at Lucas. "I'll leave you two to chat."

SIXTEEN

Isabella smiled at Lucas across the table. "It sounds like that went well."

Gigi had shared with Isabella about the guilt she'd felt in regards to Lucas and Arianna. Isabella had also known from the time she'd spent talking to Lucas that he didn't harbor any ill feelings toward Gigi, so it was wonderful to see the exchange that had obviously taken place.

"It did, yes. I always liked Gigi—especially the fact that she was intensely protective of Ari back then. I understand how difficult it probably was for her—just all of it, I mean."

"I think keeping secrets must be hard." Even as Isabella heard the words out of her mouth she did a quick mental check about any secrets that she might be keeping herself these days. Nope, all pretty good—not including the thoughts that she wasn't sharing with Thomas about Thomas.

Lucas laughed. "What's that look? Dare I ask?"

Isabella laughed too and shook her head. "Oh, nothing. Just a little drama going on inside my head."

"I'm a good listener—if you want to talk about it. And not

that people have been saying anything in particular, but I gather it has something to do with Thomas?"

Isabella crinkled her nose. "So, I guess this is what I have to look forward to now, belonging to this big family of sorts—everyone in my business." She was joking, but at the same time she couldn't help but wonder what the others had been saying.

"Oh, no, Isabella. I don't mean to imply that. No one was saying anything bad and I don't think it was about nosiness, really. Everyone just really cares about you, of course. They want you to be happy. And we all know how important your relationship—your friendship—with Thomas is to you, so that's all it is. And you don't have to tell me anything at all. We certainly have plenty of things to talk about, don't we?"

Isabella smiled and reached across the table to put her hand on Lucas's. "You know what? Maybe I would like to get your perspective on things. It's nice that you and Kate have met him—that you've spent time around the two of us together." Isabella glanced around the room until her eyes landed on Kate.

"Shall I bring Kate over to join us?" Lucas asked. "Honestly, she gives great advice. Take it from someone who's listened to her a time or two."

Isabella nodded. "Yes, please. I'm going to go refill my coffee before my therapy session begins."

Lucas laughed as he got up to go get Kate.

Isabella was lucky that she had so many people in her life who cared about her. It was unbelievable to her that she'd gone from being a girl who kept so much bottled up inside—well, apart from telling Thomas every secret she'd ever had—to being someone who was willing to be open and honest with so many people in her life that she now trusted.

As she waited for Lucas and Kate back at the table, Isabella flashed to words that Arianna had written her in so many of the letters in the journal she'd left for her daughter—words about being open and honest. Her mother had wanted some things for Isabella that she'd only known in those last few months of her life.

Even though Isabella was coming against some bumps along the way, she was determined to always keep those wishes in her mind—to not close herself off to those who loved her and maybe, more importantly, to not close herself off to true love when it made itself known to her.

Was that why she was so willing to talk to Lucas and Kate about Thomas? Maybe she wanted some kind of assurance from someone else that she wasn't crazy—that there was something other than friendship there between them.

Before she had time to dwell on what she would and wouldn't reveal, Kate was leaning down to give her a big hug.

"Isabella, we love it here so much. I'm still pinching myself that we actually made the trip. It's like a dream for all of us. And Annie—well, I'm not at all convinced that she's going to want to leave with us." Kate and Lucas both laughed as they looked over where Annie was deeply engrossed in something with her new friends.

"Well, I love having you all here—and I know I speak for everyone," said Isabella.

Kate scooted her chair in closer to Isabella's. "So, Lucas told me that you wanted to share something with us—something that's going on with you and Thomas. I did wonder if everything was okay, but I didn't want to pry."

Isabella took a deep breath and then filled Lucas and Kate in on everything that had happened since they'd last seen her in San Francisco at Thanksgiving. She told them about the night in the hotel room—about how she felt being so close with Thomas there. And she told them about the one kiss they'd shared only a week ago.

She tried not to get emotional about it as she talked, but before she could help it, Kate was handing her some tissue and putting her arm around her.

"So, as you can see, things have been a little weird between us lately. But we are talking and on the surface, everything is fine —back to normal, I suppose."

"But maybe it's not so fine with you." Kate looked at her intently.

Isabella swallowed the lump in her throat and could only nod her head, because she thought that speaking in that moment would cause her to burst into tears. She didn't want to make a commotion that would draw the attention of Lia, who was busy with her guests in the restaurant.

"Love is so tricky sometimes. I don't know why that is, but there's no other way to describe it." Kate laughed and then must have noticed a look of surprise on Isabella's face. "Okay, so regardless of where you two stand, I can use the word love because I know you two love one another as friends. Isn't that right? It sure felt that way when you were together at our house, so I don't think I'm speaking out of turn."

"No, that's a fair thing to say. And I think Thomas would agree. Really, that's why this whole thing is an issue—because we don't want to mess that up, right?"

Lucas was watching the two of them from across the table and finally he grinned at Kate. "So, are you going to tell Isabella, or should I?" He laughed.

Kate laughed too and reached down to squeeze Isabella's hand. "Go ahead." She rolled her eyes, and the whole exchange had Isabella's curiosity so piqued that her tears stopped almost immediately.

"Do tell. I feel a story coming on," said Isabella.

Lucas proceeded to tell Isabella the story of how he and Kate had met one another at a mutual friend's party and become best friends in the several months following, and how oblivious he'd been for the better part of an entire year of their hanging out with each other.

Kate's version of the story sounded much like how Isabella had always felt about Thomas. Like Isabella with Thomas, she'd greatly valued Lucas's friendship. Then one day when Lucas had been asking her advice about his current girlfriend, she looked at him and realized that she didn't want him to be with anyone else.

"And did you know then that you loved him?" Isabella asked, genuinely in awe over their story and how much her own feelings seemed to mirror the ones that Kate had been having for Lucas.

"Heck, no." Kate laughed. "Like you, it freaked me out and I didn't know what to do about how I was feeling."

Lucas laughed. "Kate pulled away from me big time and, I admit, it took me a while to figure out how much I missed her being in my life."

Isabella giggled. "Well, I guess at least one of you finally figured it out."

Kate laughed too. "Lucas finally came to his senses, asking me what was up."

"And? You told him the truth?"

"I had no choice. I was a mess, quite honestly. At that point, I figured I didn't have much to lose. Oh, I still didn't know that I loved him, but I told him that I was confused about my feelings for him. After a very awkward conversation, he called me the next day to tell me that he wanted us to go on a proper date."

Lucas laughed. "And the rest, as they say, is history."

Kate leaned over to give Lucas a kiss on the cheek before she turned back toward Isabella to finish the story. "He took me for a picnic in Golden Gate Park. We spent hours talking on a blanket before he finally kissed me""

"—And two months later during a weekend trip to Vegas, we were married." Lucas interrupted.

Isabella felt her eyes grow wide. "You eloped?"

Kate turned toward Lucas and reached out for the hand he offered her. "We sure did. And I paid a bit of a price for it from my mother, but she got over it." Kate laughed.

"I blame it on the lucky streak we'd been having. I don't really gamble much, but I'd won a few hands of poker that night and at one point I looked over at Kate, who'd been sitting beside me watching the game. I know it sounds corny to say, but I suddenly had this realization that I didn't want to lose her —not ever."

Kate laughed. "And the next thing I knew, he'd grabbed my hand and off we went to the Elvis chapel down the street."

"Well, I did ask, honey."

"That you did—right beside the bright lights of the casino slot machines outside the poker room."

Isabella laughed. "Thank you. That's an incredible story."

Kate looked at her and smiled. "I'm not saying that you're meant to be with Thomas in that way—only the two of you can figure that out." She glanced over at Lucas. "I guess our point in sharing our story with you is that being open to what life has for you is what really matters. I believe that if you're honest with

Thomas about how you feel, your relationship will work itself out—whatever ends up happening or not happening in the romance department between the two of you."

Isabella smiled and got up to hug both Kate and Lucas. "Thank you. I'm really glad that I told you both about what's been going on. I feel better—definitely much more positive about things. And by positive, I don't mean that I'm secretly planning a scheme to get Thomas to go to Vegas with me." She laughed at the look on Lucas's face.

"Hey, now. There was no scheming involved." Lucas winked and then hugged his daughter close. "I'm glad you feel better, honey."

SEVENTEEN

Lia stood in the doorway of the dining room at the villa watching everyone at the table eating and laughing—enjoying the Christmas meal she and Chase had prepared. She saw Antonio watching her from where he sat at the head of the table. He smiled that wide grin that she loved, winked, and then quietly got up from the table to come over to her. He grabbed her around the waist from behind, pulling her around the corner into the kitchen.

She felt his lips on the back of her neck, his breath warm near her ear as he whispered. "Merry Christmas, my love."

She turned around, putting her arms around his neck as she looked into his eyes. "Merry Christmas, darling. Do you have any idea how happy I am right now?"

He smiled, nodding his head. "Well, if the fact that you look possibly the most beautiful I've ever seen you look is any indication of your happiness, I'd say that you're pretty darn happy."

Lia laughed. "You say that all the time."

"That's because you get more and more beautiful—every day it surprises me more."

They kissed and Lia gently poked him in the chest. "Oh, you and your Italian charm. You do realize that you don't need to woo me anymore? You got the girl, Antonio." Lia laughed.

Antonio's face grew serious—in a teasing sort of way. "Nonsense, you will always be worthy of my charms. I will never stop trying to win your heart that much more, my love."

Lia still felt like pinching herself at times—even after being married to Antonio almost ten years. The fact that she'd had so much good in her life—Antonio, Gabriela, Thyme, the villa in Italy, and all of these people around her that she called her family—was still magical to her. She'd always be grateful for what her daughter, Arianna, had done for her. She'd always remember those final months that they'd finally had together as the most special gift of all.

Antonio squeezed her to him, whispering in her ear again. "What are you thinking about, honey? Arianna?" He pulled his head back so that he could look into her eyes.

There'd been a time in their marriage when Lia had shed tears any time they'd spoken about the daughter they'd lost. Mostly she'd felt immense guilt for the fact that Antonio had never had the chance to know her. But Antonio had been so steadfast in his determination that Lia truly feel his forgiveness, and somehow over the years it had really sunk in that Ari's real hope for her had been all about moving forward—in Italy, with the restaurant that she'd given her mother. If Arianna had known about Antonio, Lia knew that her daughter would have been beside herself with joy for what had happened between her birth parents.

Lia kissed Antonio again. "Yes, I'm thinking about Arianna, but they're all happy thoughts." She took him by the hand and pulled him back near the doorway where they had a view of everyone smiling and talking at the big dining table. "Antonio, could you ever imagine that our life could be so full —that we'd have a home here together filled with all these people we love?"

"They are pretty wonderful. And I love it when our home is full of people also. You're the most perfect hostess, and it's your touch that makes everyone feel so special here"—he kissed her on the cheek—"including your adoring husband."

Lia saw Isabella noticing them from where she sat at the table. She got up and came over to them, a big smile on her face.

"Hi, you two. Anything I can help you with? Is everything okay?"

Lia and Antonio looked at one another and smiled before Antonio removed his arm from around Lia's waist to give his granddaughter a hug. "Everything is just perfect, my dear. We were just talking about how insanely happy we were to have our home filled with all the people we love so much—especially you." Antonio kissed Isabella on the cheek. "Now, I'll leave you two so that I can get back to our guests."

Isabella put her arm around Lia's waist. "Dinner was so good. I think Lucas and Kate are feeling really spoiled by your cooking." Isabella laughed. "I swear, last time I left you guys, I dreamt about your food for weeks."

Lia leaned over to kiss Isabella on the cheek. "Last time you left, I dreamt about you for weeks, my dear. I must admit that I'm already feeling a bit sad, thinking about you all leaving."

"Aww, don't be sad. You know we'll all be back as soon as we can. I love it here so much—well, and I haven't actually decided yet what I'm doing, so you may have me for a few extra days—if that's okay." Isabella winked.

"Oh, you. You know that's more than okay. I'd love to have

you all to myself for a few days as well. We can just chill out a bit after all the festivities—maybe go to the coast for a few days."

"That sounds wonderful, actually—a very enticing offer," said Isabella. "Now what can I help you with? I think you should go sit down and enjoy some of that lovely food you've prepared."

Lia smiled. "You go sit. I'll be right there. I was just on my way to get another bottle of wine." Lia stood in the doorway for a few more seconds as she watched Isabella make her way back to the table. She smiled when she saw Annie pop up to go sit on her sister's lap the minute Isabella was seated in her chair. Isabella was laughing at something the little girl had said and they looked so sweet with their heads together.

When she and Antonio had started their marriage together at the villa, he'd promised her a home and a lifetime filled with love and laughter; he'd more than kept his promise to her as they'd watched their little family expand right before their very eyes.

Lia saw Rafael sneak a quick kiss from Jemma and she couldn't help but wonder about the two of them. Gigi had told her in private that she felt certain the two young people would end up married one day. Having known Jemma since she was a child, Lia felt as close to her as if she were her own granddaughter, and Jemma treated her and Antonio the same, always very loving and respectful of them. She could imagine a time soon when there'd be babies to cuddle and toddlers to chase around the vineyard.

She laughed at herself for having those thoughts. It was something she and Gigi talked about together—Jemma and Isabella getting married and starting families of their own—but they both knew better than to say much in front of the men in their lives. Douglas and Antonio were forever scolding the two of them for getting ahead of themselves when it came to the kids and their romantic lives.

She watched Isabella again before she headed back to the table with the bottle of wine. Her granddaughter seemed happier since she'd finally been speaking with Thomas again. Lia really didn't understand the friendship that the two seemed to have, and she was dying to meet the young man herself after everything Gigi had told her about how they seemed together. Gigi had her own ideas about that relationship too. Lia shook her head and laughed to herself as she finally made her way back to the table.

Isabella was young and had plenty of time for romance. In the meantime, Lia and Antonio, along with Emily and Richard, would do their best to support her dreams of travel and writing. It was a noble dream to help fulfill in whatever way they could. For now, Lia would enjoy every minute that she had with her beautiful granddaughter there in Italy.

EIGHTEEN

Isabella laughed as the girls tore into their presents under the tree. There were beautiful dresses and all the new dolls, games, and toys that the grown-ups had been able to get their hands on. They might have gone slightly overboard when it came to the kids, but watching their faces certainly made it all worthwhile.

She smiled at Lucas as he came to stand beside her. "I think maybe you guys are going to need to buy another piece of luggage to transport all of Annie's new gifts back with you."

Lucas laughed. "You know, I think that's actually a good plan."

"Or you can leave some of her new things here—for when you come back to visit us soon," Lia said, coming up behind them to grab Isabella in a big hug.

Lucas smiled as he looked over at Annie laughing with her mother. "Well, I'm pretty sure that wouldn't take a lot of convincing. Our time here has been really incredible." Lucas put his arm around Isabella. "It's going to seem weird not being able to see you every day."

Isabella nodded. She'd been thinking a lot lately herself—about saying her goodbyes and what was going to be next for her. She'd already spoken to her parents about the fact that she'd decided that she wasn't going back to the United States or to Harvard—at least for a while. That was the only thing she was certain about at this point.

The taste that she'd had for writing and for traveling had given her enough of a glimpse into another lifestyle that she was interested to see where it would lead. And she was also very aware of all the places still left to visit marked out on Arianna's map—it had become something of a quest in her mind, one that felt worthy of pursuit.

After talking to Gigi and Douglas, it was a toss-up right now for going to Guatemala, staying in Tuscany for a while longer, or heading out to see more of Europe. The one thing that seemed to be changing was the fact that Jemma wouldn't be joining her for anything other than the possible Guatemala trip. Isabella was still trying to fully wrap her head around the idea of traveling by herself, but deep down she knew that she could handle it now and was trying to make her decisions based on what felt right to her and not letting fear of being on her own stand in her way.

"Huh? Sorry, Lia. What was that?"

Lia laughed. "Wow, you seemed a million miles away just now. Everything okay?"

Lucas looked at her too, waiting for her response.

"Oh, yeah. I was just thinking about what it is I'm going to do next. I suppose I'll need to be making a decision soon."

"Well, it's certainly no rush on our part. You know that your grandfather and I would love for you to stay as long as you're able to."

Isabella kissed Lia on the cheek. "I know. And that's really sweet. Well, whatever I end up doing, I won't be staying away for long—and that goes for you guys too." She nodded at Lucas. "I'd love to come back to San Francisco again in the near future when we'd have more time to spend together there."

"That sounds like a perfect idea to me." Lucas gave her one more squeeze before heading across the room to see what wonderful new present Annie was squealing about.

Lia excused herself to go talk to Antonio about something, and Isabella caught Jemma's eye from across the room.

Jemma grinned, kissed Rafael on the cheek, and then disappeared outside the door for a few seconds before coming back towards Isabella with a big box full of wrapped gifts in her arms.

Isabella laughed and met her across the room to help carry what looked like a heavy load.

"Oh, Jem. Everyone is going to love their gifts from you. I can't wait to see their faces." Isabella peered into the box, noticing a smaller one than all the rest right on top. She raised an eyebrow. "Is that a new one I see?" She'd watched Jemma create every painting throughout their travels.

Jemma nodded, a big grin on her face. "It's for Raf. I've done it since he arrived here."

Isabella watched her friend's face go red as she whispered to her.

"It's one I did from a picture of myself here, actually—the one you took of me in the vineyard. I figured it might be something nice that he can remember this trip by."

"Oh, he's going to love that."

"And what about you? Where are your gifts?"

"They're just tucked away behind the chair over there. You go first."

Jemma handed out her paintings to the delight of everyone. Somehow she'd even managed the time to do one of the vineyard for Lucas and Kate. She walked over to Isabella, handing her a gift that was smaller than most of the others.

"Jem—you kept one hidden from me, I see."

Jemma laughed. "I did this one while you were away to San Francisco for Thanksgiving. I made it smaller in case you want to travel with it—oh, but don't feel like you have to or anything."

Isabella laughed as she tore the paper off her gift. "Oh, wow!"

It was the recreation of a selfie that Jemma had taken of the two girls after they'd walked up the steps of the Duomo in Florence. It was the first stop on their journey together. Jemma had perfectly captured in her painting the same excited expressions apparent on their faces in that photo.

Isabella threw her arms around her friend's neck in a big hug. "Ooh, of course I'll want to take it with me. I love it so much."

Jemma grinned back at her. "Okay it's your turn. I can't wait to see what everyone thinks when you give them your gifts."

Isabella grinned back at her and then went to retrieve her own hidden box of wrapped gifts behind the chair in the living room, where everyone was still chatting. She handed them out one by one, amused at the looks on their faces. Whenever anyone had asked her how her writing was coming, she'd been very noncommittal about it, saying that she was enjoying the process and making good headway on the book. No one, besides Jemma and Thomas, knew that her book had already been published, and she couldn't wait to let them know.

"Bella!" Gigi was the first to see the cover and immediately came to give her a big hug and kiss. "You sneaky girl, you. I had no idea." She laughed.

Blu was grinning and then read out loud from the cover, "*Her Mother's Eyes*—Isabella Dawson—Bella, this is fantastic. I can't wait to read it."

Lia and Antonio both came over to where Isabella stood as she brushed the tears away from her eyes. The room got quiet as Lia opened the book and began reading the dedication page out loud.

"To my family, which has grown in numbers that I never would have imagined. Thank you more than words can say, for all the love and support you've given me. And to Arianna—this book is a tribute to you. I will be forever grateful for the legacy you've left me and for making all my dreams come true." Lia finished with tears streaming down her face as she and Antonio hugged Isabella and told her how proud they were of her.

The room erupted in noise and shouts as everyone made their way over to hug and congratulate Isabella.

Isabella felt incredibly happy and very proud in that moment. It had been quite an accomplishment, and she truly felt that so much of her heart and soul had gone into the writing—that it didn't even matter to her if it sold any copies or not. What mattered to her most was the love and support from everyone there in that room, and she knew that she'd always have that.

Amidst the chatter and the sounds of the children playing a loud game in the corner, Isabella could hear her phone ringing where she'd placed it on the table near Jemma earlier. "Jem, will you see who that is, please?"

Jemma, with a wide grin on her face, held up Isabella's

phone to her so that she could see Thomas's face on the screen. "Bella, take it."

Isabella grabbed the phone and walked out into the foyer where it was quiet. She studied Thomas as she looked into the screen. "Hey, you. Merry Christmas. Where are you? It's so dark?"

Thomas laughed. "Iz, come to the front door."

"What? Thomas, don't kid me."

"Come. Open the door."

He was grinning at her and Isabella felt her heart race as she took the few quick steps that had her across the foyer and opening the front door. She saw Thomas standing in front of her holding what looked like mistletoe above his head and before she could say a word, he'd pulled her to him. His lips were on hers and she couldn't think as she let herself enjoy the pure bliss of his kiss for what felt like several minutes.

Finally, he put his head back a bit so that she could look into his eyes.

"Merry Christmas, Iz," he said.

And then he kissed her again.

NINETEEN

Isabella's heart was racing. This had to be a dream—and most definitely a dream that she didn't want to wake up from. She opened her eyes as their lips parted again, taking in everything about this man who held her in his arms. It was Thomas—her Thomas—her best friend—and she knew in that moment that she never wanted to leave his arms. Everything about it felt right to her—like coming home to a place that was pure comfort.

"Thomas, what are you doing here?" Isabella finally spoke, her voice barely a whisper.

He laughed at her as he looked into her eyes and took her hand firmly in his own. "I couldn't be away from you. I needed to see you." He leaned in to kiss her again. "Can we sit down somewhere and talk?"

"Yes, of course. Oh, I can't wait for you to meet everyone. Let's go inside."

"We will, but first I want you to myself for a few minutes more. There are some things I need to say to you, my darling."

Isabella grinned. It was a familiar term of endearment that Thomas had been using with her for years, but it felt different to her now—different in the way that she sensed their whole relationship was about to shift.

Thomas took his coat off and put it around Isabella's shoulders.

She squeezed his hand and led him around the corner of the house to the terrace. It was private. They could still hear everyone inside, but they were shielded from their view.

"Oh, maybe I should pop in and let them know we're out here—so Lia doesn't worry, I mean."

"I'm pretty sure that Jemma will fill her in," said Thomas grinning—probably at the look Isabella must have had on her face. "I needed some help in planning this, you know."

"And how long have you been planning this little surprise?"

Thomas sat down on one of the chairs at the table, pulling Isabella down into the chair beside him. "I'll get to that."

Isabella loved the look she saw on his face. It was his normal mischievous look, one that was as familiar to her as her own features in the mirror—but there was something more—something that she didn't think she'd seen before. And it made her heart race.

Thomas turned his chair so that he was knee-to-knee with Isabella, facing her. He reached for both her hands, holding them tight.

Isabella smiled but she was having a hard time keeping eye contact with him.

"Iz, don't freak out on me." Thomas brought one of her hands to his lips.

She laughed lightly. "I'm not. I'm just—well, somewhat shocked, I guess. In a good way, I mean."

"I figured you would be. But I hope that you're as happy to see me as I am to see you."

He leaned forward to give her a quick kiss on the lips, and Isabella wondered how it was that his lips already felt so familiar to her—like she'd been kissing him all her life.

He squeezed her hands again and looked her in the eyes. "I have some things I want to say to you, Isabella Dawson."

She nodded and laughed. "So you've said. Go on then."

"Well, firstly it wasn't true what I'd told you about the kiss we shared—back in London."

"Not true about which part?"

"I think I probably made it sound like I'd never thought of kissing you before that night…"

Isabella looked at him, sitting across from her, feeling him on the verge of telling her everything she'd ever wanted to hear. She knew what he was going to say before he'd uttered the words.

"In San Francisco?" Her voice was still a whisper. Maybe she was afraid that somehow this spell they seemed under could still break—that sitting there so close to Thomas, the feel of his lips on hers still so familiar, could go away in the blink of an eye if she wasn't careful.

Thomas smiled and brought her hand to his lips once again. "Yes, it was in San Francisco—while we were on the bridge, while we were shopping downtown, when you were lying in my lap during our movie night that last night. I think I'd been kidding myself for months, Iz. Telling myself that it—that you and I—weren't possible—not like that—not as a couple. But—"

Isabella didn't miss it when Thomas let go of her hand to run his own through his hair. It was that thing he always did when he was feeling nervous, and now as she watched him she felt herself smiling, on the one hand wanting to tease him as she always did, but on the other recognizing that it was a time to be serious—more serious than they'd ever been with one another.

"But?" Isabella whispered, looking into Thomas's eyes as he reached for both her hands again.

He leaned forward and gave her the kiss she'd been wanting again—this time it was longer, and when he pulled away slightly to look into her eyes, she knew that his next words were going to be everything she'd ever wanted to hear.

"The truth is, I love you. I'm in love with you, Izzy."

"Really?" She felt the tears stinging her eyes and the next thing she knew Thomas's finger was gently brushing the wetness away; a second later, his lips were gentle on her cheek, her eyelid, her lips once again.

He pulled away, laughing a little. "Please tell me those are happy tears and not tears of horror."

Isabella could only shake her head, not trusting herself to speak with all of the emotion that seemed to be caught in her throat as she reached for his neck, pulling him to her for the hug and scent of his cologne that was so familiar to her. Finally before they had the chance to break apart again, she whispered in his ear.

"I love you too."

Now he created the distance necessary to look her in the eyes, his smile wide, the question gone from his face. He nodded. "Yeah?"

Isabella laughed before she gave him a quick kiss on the lips. "I think I've always loved you."

Thomas pulled her to his lap, Isabella's head perfectly falling against his chest, where they sat quietly for several minutes before Thomas finally brought her face to his for another kiss. He led her gently back to her chair as he stood up to retrieve something from his backpack that he'd set off to the side earlier.

"I've got a little present for you," he said, smiling at what must have been a look of surprise on Isabella's face.

"What? Thomas, no. You already gave me my present—the journal in London—and I don't have anything else for you—if that's what you're hoping." She laughed.

"Oh, well, if you don't want it..." Thomas made a motion to put the small package back into his bag.

"Hey, don't you dare, mister." Isabella laughed.

Thomas kissed her again before he put the small wrapped gift into her hands. "And by the way, those sweet kisses are the only present I ever need from you."

Isabella's head went back a bit as she laughed, and she could feel his lips gentle on her neck, landing just under her ear and practically making her lose her breath for the way he was making her feel.

She looked at him as she felt the small gift in her hand, holding it up to give it a small shake, laughing as she did so. "Is it the keys to a new car, that new key chain I've been wanting, a gift certificate for the mall back home..."

"Just open it." Thomas was grinning at her, obviously enjoying her teasing.

Isabella smiled as she peeled off the paper and tentatively opened the lid of the velvet box. "Oh, Thomas! You didn't! It's so beautiful."

Thomas lifted the diamond necklace out of the box as Isabella turned around and moved her hair off her neck to her shoulder. She first felt the lightest of kisses along the side of her neck before his fingers gently secured the perfect band of small diamonds around her neck. She felt his breath on her ear before she turned around so that he could admire the beautiful gift he'd given her.

"You, Isabella Dawson, are a woman worthy of diamonds."

She turned to face him, her lips finding his, her fingers gently reaching to touch the gift that so perfectly suited the neckline of the dress she was wearing. "Thank you." And she wondered if he'd noticed.

Thomas stepped back a bit, and she could feel him taking her in from head to toe, his eyes lingering where the necklace didn't quite touch the material of the dress that fit her as if it were made for her alone. He kissed her again quickly. "I think this just might be your lucky dress."

She grinned up at him. "You noticed."

"I can't forget how you looked that night—the night of our first kiss, Bella." He pulled her to him, kissing her again and again with quick gentle kisses on her lips. "And now our second kiss and more kisses that I want to lose track of for kissing those lips of yours over and over again."

Isabella laughed, looking up at him in the moonlight. "Hey, you called me Bella."

"You are—my lovely, perfect Bella."

TWENTY

Lia watched Isabella and Thomas make their way across the room hand-in-hand to where everyone stood awaiting the introductions. Her granddaughter looked blissfully happy. Anyone could see that, Lia thought as she felt Antonio's arms draw her in closer to where he stood. She reached up to give her husband a quick peck on the cheek. "Our Isabella looks lovely, doesn't she?"

Antonio nodded, kissing the top of Lia's head. "She sure does. I'd say that young man is lucky that he's finally come to his senses."

Isabella came over to give first Lia and then Antonio a kiss on the cheek. "Lia, Antonio—everyone, this is Thomas."

"Thomas!" Annie shouted at the top of her lungs, running from across the room to hurl herself at Thomas's legs causing everyone to burst out laughing.

Thomas reached down to pick the little girl up, bringing her to eye level. "Hey there, Annie. Nice to see you again so soon. Are you having a good Christmas?"

Annie nodded. "The best." She put her arms around his

neck, giving him a big hug. "Thomas, can you please put me down now? I have to go back to play with my friends," she said, pointing to where Gabriela and Kylie sat on the floor totally consumed with the Christmas gifts they'd just opened.

"Well, someone sure does seem to give you the full approval." Antonio stuck out his hand toward Thomas. "Thomas, we're glad you could make it."

"Thank you for having me, sir."

"Please call me Antonio, and this is my wife, Lia."

Thomas leaned in to give Lia a kiss on the cheek. "I've heard so many great things about you both—and this place, which seems pretty amazing even in the dark." He laughed.

Lia didn't miss the tightening of Isabella's hand as Thomas looked toward her granddaughter and then pulled her gently closer by his side. She thought the two looked perfect together—and Isabella possibly happier than she'd ever seen her. Lia's eyes went to Isabella's neck.

"Oh, honey. That is gorgeous."

Isabella's hand went to her necklace and Lia didn't miss the flush to her cheeks. It was an extravagant gift—something given to someone who was much more than just a friend.

"It is, isn't it? Maybe a bit much, but—"

"But nothing." Thomas winked. "A beautiful gift for a beautiful woman."

Lia saw Thomas's eyes go toward Emily and Richard as they walked across the room toward the small group.

"Mr. and Mrs. Dawson." Thomas reached out his hand toward Richard, who promptly drew him in for a big hug.

"Thomas, it's great to see you."

Lia thought Isabella looked slightly embarrassed as she saw her let go of Thomas's hand to hug her mother.

"Mom, can you believe Thomas came all the way here to surprise me?"

Emily reached down to touch Isabella's necklace and they were close enough that Lia could hear her whisper in her daughter's ear. "The necklace looks beautiful on you, honey, and I take it you and Thomas have made up?"

Isabella laughed and nodded just as Jemma came behind her to wrap her arms around her neck.

"Bella, what do you think of your surprise?"

"I think you are the worst friend ever for keeping secrets from me!" Isabella said before laughing and whispering something in Jemma's ear that Lia couldn't hear.

Thomas greeted Gigi and Douglas and met Blu, Chase, and Rafael before Lia scooted everyone back into the living room for hot chocolate and dessert, pulling Isabella aside for a minute to hand her the one ornament that she'd set aside earlier that week.

"I'd gotten this one for Thomas, before I knew that he wasn't able to make it."

"Oh, wow. Thank you." Isabella hugged her, but not before she saw the tears in her granddaughter's eyes. "I really love him, Lia."

Lia looked at Isabella, standing in front of her, so poised and beautiful; and out of the corner of her eye, she didn't miss the expression on Thomas's face as he watched her granddaughter too. "I'm pretty sure that he loves you too."

"Bella, how wonderful that your Thomas is here." Gigi winked as she came up beside Isabella and Lia, reaching her arm around Isabella's waist. "And let me see that magnificent necklace, sweet girl."

Isabella giggled at Gigi's words and the scrutiny of the gift around her neck. "I guess he just might be my Thomas after all."

"Well, it's good to know that he has the sense that we all gave him credit for." Gigi laughed too. "You better go over there before those girls get him wrapped up in their little tea party they've got going on at the table."

Lia and Gigi linked arms as they watched Isabella cross the room to whisper something in Thomas's ear before handing him the ornament with his name on it. He looked over at Lia, giving her a big grin before he walked to the Christmas tree to place his ornament next to Isabella's. Then she watched him turn toward her granddaughter and give her the sweetest of kisses. It was a kiss that said just the right amount about his feelings while being polite enough to acknowledge there were others in the room keenly aware of the change in the young couple's status.

Gigi turned toward Lia with a big grin. "I have a good feeling about this, Lia."

Lia nodded, also smiling. "Me too, Gigi. Me too."

TWENTY-ONE

Isabella felt Thomas grab her hand under the table. She smiled and leaned over to give him a light kiss on the cheek. They were meeting Jemma and Rafael at Thyme for one last meal together before they left with Gigi and Douglas for Florence in the afternoon. The four of them were catching a flight to Guatemala in the morning, and Isabella and Thomas would be staying on at the villa for a few more days.

Thomas scooted his chair closer, looking quickly around the quiet restaurant before giving Isabella a long full kiss on the mouth. She felt the sigh escape her lips without even being aware of it until it had happened. She giggled right next to his lips and smiled as he pulled away just a little bit to look at her.

"Are you happy, Iz?"

The expression on his face told her that he knew that she was.

"Insanely so. Can't you tell?" she teased him back.

"I can tell. I can always tell when you're happy."

His look went from silly to serious, and Isabella's heart

tugged at the way it made her feel. She really did love this man. It felt good to admit it—to herself and to him. And to be loved by him? She was still in a state of shock about everything that had happened between them.

"It's been a great Christmas, hasn't it?" Isabella asked.

"The best. Seriously, I'm so glad I came."

"You're glad?" Isabella laughed. "I'm still in shock."

"It was a great surprise, wasn't it?"

"The best surprise." Isabella smiled at him. "And I can't believe that you've finally met my whole family."

"And I adore them all. Honestly, Lia and Antonio—the vineyard, this restaurant—it's all been just how you'd described, only a hundred times better." He leaned over to give her another kiss. "—And especially the part about my getting to finally kiss you again here in Italy."

Isabella laughed, kissing him back. "Well, yes, that part has been pretty nice for me too."

Before she could return Thomas's kiss with one of her own, she noticed Jemma waving as she and Rafael walked up to the door of the restaurant.

"Hey, you two." Jemma walked through the door, making her way over to give Isabella a hug. "Can you believe how gorgeous the weather is today?"

"Maybe you guys should postpone your flight and stay here with us a few more days?" Isabella grinned but she already assumed she knew the answer.

Jemma glanced at Rafael, who'd pulled out her chair for her. "Oh, we'd love to, but Raf needs to get back to work."

They settled in at the table, giving their coffee order to the waitress.

Isabella reached for her friend's hand. "Jem, I'm not quite

sure what I'm going to do without you every day. You've been such a constant in my life these past months. It already feels weird to me."

"Well, I'm pretty sure this one's gonna do a good job of taking my place." Jemma gestured toward Thomas and winked. "So tell us your plans. Where are you two headed?"

Isabella grinned as she looked first at Thomas and then back to Jemma. "Well, we've got about seven months until Thomas needs to be back to start at NYU. We figure we'll spend a bit more time in Italy and then Paris."

"Ah, back to the city of love." Jemma was grinning at her, and Isabella felt her cheeks flush.

When she and Thomas had talked about where they wanted to travel together, he'd brought up Paris and even though Isabella had already been there, it seemed the perfect place to go back to—to experience with him. She was already envisioning dining at the Eiffel Tower and long walks through her favorite park.

Isabella felt Thomas reach for her hand underneath the table.

"I feel that Iz deserves some serious romance after what I've put her through." Thomas was looking at her intently. "And really, what I've put us both through."

"What do you mean?" Rafael asked.

"We should have been together months ago, but I was too thick-headed to realize it."

"Well, you're together now and that's what matters," said Jemma.

Thomas leaned over to give Isabella a quick kiss on the cheek just as he'd done a hundred times before during the course of their friendship, but as Isabella felt her stomach flutter and she saw the look in his eyes, she knew that everything was completely different between them now.

Isabella grinned as she squeezed Thomas's hand underneath the table and looked at Jemma, with Rafael's arm around her. "Yep. We're together now. And that's what matters."

THE STORY CONTINUES

Bella's Heart
Legacy Series, Book 9

Available on Amazon

PaulaKayBooks.com

BELLA'S HEART — PREVIEW

Chapter 1

Isabella gave a start in her chair at the feel of Thomas's hand on her back.

"Hey. How was your walk?" she asked. "You were out early this morning."

Thomas leaned down to give her a quick kiss on the lips before he sat in the chair next to her. "Great. Would you believe that I jogged a little?"

"Did you?" Isabella got up from her own chair to sit on Thomas's lap, wrapping her arms around his neck and teasing him with her smile. "Does that mean you're ready to go for a run with me? I was just about to take a break."

"Were you now?" Thomas leaned in to give her a deep kiss, momentarily causing her to forget any ideas about running or finishing the current chapter she was writing.

Isabella moved back into her own chair and reached for Thomas's hand across the small table as she looked out toward the sea. "I'm still in awe of our view here." She felt the familiar ache that she'd been having lately at the thought of their travels ending. "Thomas, are we really going to leave our little island paradise next week?"

Thomas looked at her intently before replying to the question that Isabella already knew the answer to.

Traveling with Thomas the past seven months had been a dream. From the moment he'd surprised her at the villa over Christmas—from the moment he'd finally kissed her again—the two had been inseparable. It had been just like old times with her best friend, only everything was different.

Thomas loved her, and it was in a way that made everything magical and intense for Isabella.

Spending time in Paris again had been incredible and romantic. Isabella had put her writing on hold to do all the tourist things she hadn't done the first time around. And then they'd gone on to Spain and Portugal, the weeks turning into months, their travels taking them to Eastern Europe and then Turkey.

They'd decided to end their time traveling together with a month long stay in Greece, and Isabella was loving everything about her time in Santorini. She'd finally gotten back into a morning writing groove and her afternoons with Thomas had been spent lounging at the beach, eating delicious Mediterranean salads and talking about everything they'd seen and done.

Isabella turned her attention back to Thomas, who was nudging her gently in the side.

"Huh? Sorry, what was that?"

He laughed as he brought her hair back and kissed her neck just below her ear in a way that always made her forget her thoughts momentarily.

He reached for her hand and turned her just slightly in his lap so that it was easier for Isabella to look him in the eye.

"I was just saying that you don't have to leave, Iz. It's me that needs to return to New York next week—to the grind of hitting the books again—but I hate for you to give up your tra—"

"Stop." Isabella's voice interrupted Thomas right before she planted a kiss squarely on his mouth. "I am going back with you. We've already decided." She studied him intently for a few seconds.

It was shocking how attracted she was to this man who had been such a big part of her life for so many years. She still had to pinch herself at times that the two of them had actually taken such a huge leap in their relationship. He was the same goofy Thomas who'd always made her laugh, who'd always practically known her thoughts before she'd even uttered a word. Yet, so much had changed.

In the months that they'd been together as more than just friends, sometimes Isabella had to force the doubts away. Way in the back of her mind was the tiniest idea that she could wake up one day to realize that it wasn't the same for Thomas as it was for her. That she wasn't, in fact, the love of his life—not in the same way that she was sure he was for her.

But she had no reason to think that. Thomas had done nothing but reassure her of the intensity of his feelings, and she loved him all the more for knowing that she needed that from him.

"But?" Thomas kissed the tip of her nose.

"But what?"

"I know there's a but there, Iz, so just tell me what it is." He laughed, but Isabella's heart was racing slightly and she felt very serious all of a sudden.

She looked him in the eye. "Thomas, do you want me to come to New York? I mean, you'd tell me if you didn't, right?" She held her breath in as she waited for him to answer her.

It wasn't that they hadn't had lengthy discussions about it —they had. Somewhere between graduating high school and during the months of his travels with Isabella, Thomas had suddenly become more serious than he'd ever been about school. It was a side of him that Isabella hadn't really seen before—not while they'd been in high school together, anyway. It was she who was the more studious one, while Thomas hadn't really put any pressure on himself when it came to homework and his grades.

But Thomas was naturally smart, and getting into NYU had seemed to mature him in ways that were attractive to Isabella. It was quite the role reversal actually—somewhat amusing when she really stopped to think about it. When she'd brought up the subject of Thomas postponing school to travel longer, she'd found out just how serious he was, and she couldn't fault him for it.

Thomas pulled her toward him and Isabella nestled her face close under his chin, as he squeezed her tighter. "Iz, of course I want you there with me. That's not a question at all. The idea of not being able to see you every day disturbs me greatly." He laughed.

"Really?" She turned in his lap again so she could see his face.

"Really. But..."

"Oh, I see. Now, who's the one with a but, mister?" Her

voice was light, but inside she felt concern. Was there a but about her going back to New York with him?

"Come on, Iz. I just want to be sure it's what you want. I'd hate to think that you'd be giving up your dreams of travel for me. I mean, that's a lot of pressure for a guy." He laughed. "I'm not at all sure what it's going to be like, but you've already said that you want to get your own place—that you don't want us to live together—so I'm not really sure how much actual time we'll be able to spend together."

They had discussed living together. It was Thomas who'd suggested it. After all, they were living together now during their travels, he'd said. But, for whatever reason, Isabella was old-fashioned when it came to that part of their relationship—the physical part. They'd been affectionate with one another and she loved how affectionate he was with her, but Isabella wasn't ready for that next step yet.

When she'd told Thomas that a big part of her wanted to wait—maybe even until she was married one day—he'd kissed her so sweetly and told her that he loved her—that he loved everything about her. She knew that Thomas wouldn't pressure her whether they lived together or not, but she couldn't see the point of making it more difficult on either of them; and living together in a real long-term New York apartment felt a little too much like playing house to her.

So they'd decided that Isabella would stay with him—just at first—while she figured out her own living situation. She hadn't exactly expressed her own doubts to Thomas—everything had changed so quickly that her head was still swimming with all that had happened. She didn't doubt their relationship, but when it came to her actually living in New York, she'd be lying to herself if she said that she was completely comfortable with the idea. She could write from anywhere, and the large inheritance that she'd received from her birth mother—from Arianna —allowed her the freedom to give it a try anyway. So there didn't seem to be a reason not to—not when she couldn't bear the thought of being on her own, without Thomas, after so many wonderful memories they had from their travels together.

She turned her attention back to Thomas, who seemed to be waiting for some kind of reply from her. She'd been so scattered lately. Had there been a question?

"Sorry, what did you say?"

Thomas laughed. "Babe, you really are a million miles away this morning." He moved her gently off his lap. "I was just saying that we don't really know what my schedule is going to be like with school and everything. I just don't want you to be disappointed if I don't have much time to spend with you during the week, ya know?"

Isabella nodded. "I know. I do get that. We won't know until we try it, I guess. Right?"

"That's right." Thomas leaned over to give her a quick kiss on the lips. "And now, my darling, I am going to go grab a quick shower. Are you gonna go for that run?"

Isabella grinned. "Yep. I think a run will clear this cloudy distracted brain of mine. Then do you want to hit the beach with me afterward—lunch and a swim?"

"It's a date."

Chapter 2

Isabella took long even breaths in as she listened to the sound of her feet hitting the dirt trail. She'd been delighted to discover a path from their villa that led down and along the sea for a good three miles in one direction. She was finally getting to the point where she could almost complete the six miles there and back without slowing to a walk—something that would have been a piece of cake for her a year ago.

Both she and Thomas had been loving their time in Santorini. It really was as magical and picturesque as what she'd imagined when they'd booked their stay in the villa. The buildings were a crisp white against the backdrop of so many beautiful shades of blue—the dark blue domes that topped the structures, the turquoise blue of the clear sea, and the unclouded light blue of the sky. Yes, their Greek island stay had been everything she'd hoped for and more.

Isabella felt her heart lurch as it always did lately when she thought of leaving. She loved the way things had been between her and Thomas throughout their travels together. Going back to New York signified going back to real life—or at least a new reality for them both—and she didn't want their little romance bubble to burst.

She wished that she could express her fears to Thomas but something stopped her. She didn't want to be needy or untrusting, but inside she still couldn't completely accept the fact that what had happened between them wasn't going to go away. And deep down she felt herself holding back a bit for the fear of it.

She shook her head as if doing so would push any negative thoughts away as she began to make her way up the one challenging part of the trail. As she reached the top of incline, she saw the bright pink of a woman's baseball cap in the distance just before the woman stumbled and fell to the ground, her speed seeming to catapult her off the trail a good distance as she fell forward.

Isabella took off at full speed as soon as she realized what she'd seen, crossing the distance between them in seconds.

"Are you okay?" She peered down at the woman now in a sitting position with her hands around her ankle.

"Oh, hey. I'll bet that looked graceful." She laughed and then seemed to wince slightly as she looked up at Isabella.

Isabella carefully took the few steps needed to bend down next to her, eyeing the ankle that was already very swollen and a light shade of purple. "Do you think it's broken?" She reached into the small bag she wore to pull out the little first aid kit she carried with her—pretty much at all times. Thomas had teased her about it, right before he'd kissed her and said that it was kinda nice to see some of the "always prepared Izzy" that he'd known from back home.

"How annoying. That will teach me not to run and play with my music at that same time."

Isabella reached down to offer the woman her hand. "Do you want to try to stand? See if you can put any weight on it at all?" She smiled as the woman reached up to take her hand. "I'm Is—I'm Bella, by the way."

Isabella leaned down to put her other hand around the woman's shoulder, giving her more support as she stood up.

"Thanks. And I'm Nina." She winced again as she allowed Isabella to help her into a standing position.

"Good to meet you, Nina. I wish it were under better circumstances." She squeezed Nina's hand. "Okay, now lean into me if you need to and let's just see if you can put any weight at all on your foot. Take your time."

Nina gingerly put her foot down in front of her, then let it take most of her weight as she stepped forward with the other.

"Okay, it's painful, but it doesn't seem to be broken, thank God."

Isabella nodded her head, noticing the blood dripping down Nina's leg. "Okay. That's great. Do you think you can make it to that big rock over there? I have something to clean your scrape and I just happen to have a bandage that we can use to wrap your ankle."

Nina laughed. "You're really prepared, aren't you?"

"I guess I am." Isabella laughed too. "Well, I've been traveling a bit and I wasn't too sure about the things that I'd be needing while away from home."

The two made their way over to the big boulder and Nina sat down with her leg stretched out in front of her. Isabella knelt down, pouring some water from her water bottle unto the scrape just below Nina's knee. She reached into her bag, pulling out a small container of alcohol and the biggest band-aid she had, and carefully cleaned the scrape before applying the band-aid.

Nina seemed to be studying her carefully. "I feel pretty lucky that you happened to be behind me on the trail today. I just arrived here yesterday but someone from my hotel told me that it can be pretty quiet out on this trail."

"It's true. I run here nearly every day—well, for the past three weeks or so. Hmm, there's a little cafe just around the next corner down toward the beach. Do you think you can make it that far? Is there someone we can call to pick you up?"

"Yes, I think I'll be fine to walk and no, there's no one to come pick me up. I'm flying solo these days—footloose and fancy free, I guess you could say." She laughed lightly.

"Great. Well, let me wrap this bandage around your ankle.

That should help give you some support, and then we really do need to get some ice on it right away."

"You look pretty young to be a doctor." Nina winked.

Isabella laughed. "Four years of track—with my own share of injuries." She tucked the clasp into the fabric of the bandage. "There, how does that feel?"

Nina stood up and carefully hobbled a few steps. "Okay. So, I'm not gonna win any races, but maybe I'll be okay to actually enjoy some time at the beach—one can hope, anyway."

Isabella moved back to where Nina had been on the ground to collect her MP3 player and her one sneaker, before the two made their way slowly along the path. "Well, I hope this won't ruin your vacation. How long are you here for?"

"Oh, well, it's not really a vacation. I mean, it is, but sort of a working one, I guess you'd say."

"Oh? Can I ask what you do? That sounds interesting, and I suppose it's been something I've been trying out for myself."

"I'm a photographer—and a bit of a travel blogger, but mostly it's about the images for me. And it's fairly new for me too."

Isabella tried to study Nina discreetly. She felt drawn to her —fascinated about this woman, who in just a few words, seemed to stir up all kinds of emotions and questions within her. If she had to guess, she'd say that Nina seemed to be in her early thirties. She was tanned and looked to be in very good shape. There was something about her—about the way that she had laughed despite the obvious pain and frustration she'd been in earlier—that made Isabella want to know more about her.

"I'd love to hear more about what you do—if you don't mind. It sounds very interesting to me."

"Sure. Let me buy you a coffee and we'll swap stories while

we get some ice on this bad boy. You seem so young. I'd love to hear what you're doing at this little piece of paradise—and for weeks at that? I get the feeling that you're not on the average gap year backpacking trip with your buddies."

Isabella smiled as the last months flashed through her mind —getting that first phone call from Douglas, meeting her grandparents and her wonderful new extended family in Italy, and all of the many hours she'd sat reading and rereading her birth mother's journals.

No, she certainly hadn't been on just any ordinary budget backpacking trip. Isabella's whole world as she knew it had shifted, thanks to a mother she'd never had the chance to know —thanks to Arianna and her dreams for a daughter she'd only held for a moment as an infant.

Her thoughts turned toward Thomas and their upcoming move to New York as she sent him a quick text.

And her whole world was about to shift again, and for some reason, Isabella didn't know how she was feeling about that.

A NOTE FROM THE AUTHOR

Thank you so much for reading *Bella's Holiday*.

If you've fallen in love with these characters and the world of the Legacy Series, I'd love to invite you deeper into the story.

I've written a quiet, emotional prequel titled *Out of Time* that sheds light on the relationships, choices, and moments that shaped everything that follows.

As a thank-you for joining my reader list, you can receive *Out of Time* as a free digital gift, along with future updates and special releases from the Legacy Series and my other women's fiction.

To receive your free prequel, please visit:
PaulaKayBooks.com

I'm so glad you're here.
—Paula

ABOUT THE AUTHOR

Paula Kay writes women's fiction about family, friendship, and the quiet moments that shape who we become.

Her Legacy Series explores love, loss, and the ties that bind us across generations, with settings inspired by Italy, San Francisco, and the places that feel like home long after we've left them behind.

When she's not writing, Paula enjoys meaningful conversations, books that make her cry, and a little too much reality television.

PaulaKayBooks.com

ALSO BY PAULA KAY

Legacy Series:

Book 1: *Buying Time*

Book 2: *In Her Own Time*

Book 3: *Matter of Time*

Book 4: *Taking Time*

Book 5: *Just in Time*

Book 6: *All in Good Time*

Book 7: *Bella's Hope*

Book 8: *Bella's Holiday*

Book 9: *Bella's Heart*

Book 10: *Bella's Home*

Book 11: *Christmas in Tuscany: A Legacy Series Reunion*

Book 12: *Birthday Surprise: A Legacy Series Reunion*

Book 13: *A Summer Together: A Legacy Series Reunion*

Book 14: *In This Moment: A Legacy Series Reunion*

Book 15: *Where It Began: A Legacy Series Reunion*

The Nomadic Sisterhood:

Know by Heart

Stay the Course

Clear the Air

Lost for Words

Out of Touch

Turn the Tide

Rock the Boat

Back on Track